INFINITE ASTRONAUTS:

The Theory of Everything

INFINITE ASTRONAUTS:
The Theory of Everything

Mike Brumfield

Infinite Astronauts: The Theory of Everything
By Mike Brumfield
Copyright © 2011 by Mike Brumfield

ISBN 978-0-97404390-4-6

Library of Congress Catalog Card Number (Applied For)

Retail $17.95 plus $2.50 shipping.
Expect delivery in two to three weeks.
To order call 931/261-3328.

First Edition, July 2011

MICHAEL

HELLO, EVERYONE, my name is Mike Brumfield and this is my answer to the "THEORY OF EVERYTHING." It is non-fiction and my final book on this subject matter, which is simply the mystery of mankind. "THINK INFINITELY" is your first clue. Good luck! The previous six books I've written are fiction, based on real events and presented as a continuous storyline. But believe me, this one is as real as it gets.

Unbeknownst to me, for the last twenty-two years, I have been on a long, hard journey of discovery to solve mankind's mystery. The reality that I was searching overtook me about twelve years ago, and I haven't stopped since. I can't even begin to tell you all that I've learned, but I will gladly share my huge ignorance of life and these experiences, in hopes of inspiring everyone to do the same. There really is no truer saying than "a good dose of humility can go a long way." It did for me. Life is truly a "NEVER ENDING" work in progress and extremely complicated. But, I do firmly believe that humility, forgiveness, and love can conquer all our egos as well as this mystery, if we let it.

I know this all too well, now, as I have experienced all three, and a whole lot of shame, in trying to do so. It finally worked, though. I don't know everything! "THANK GOD." I still, really want to be a neurosurgeon, or at least a rock star, anyway. Just kidding! Sure the world is full of know-it-alls, but do they know rocket science? (Got 'em, huh, LOL!) Well, in all seriousness, I would like to teach kids about our universe. I think it would satisfy me much, much, more, and in fact would make me feel a whole lot better about myself, for helping mankind educate ourselves. We can all agree that knowledge is power and teaching kids is a noble "SERVICE." Anyway, thankfully, I've discovered that learning is fun, "IF YOU CAN LET YOURSELF DISCOVER IT." Love and laughter, especially at ourselves, can help us to achieve it and I hope we will all cry tears of joy when we ask, "What enemies"? We can't have them when we love everyone! Maybe we can bottle that someday. LOVE! Enjoy reading my story.

MICHAEL

While I obsessively travelled down an eye-awakening and yet very tumultuous road of seemingly endless shocking discoveries, I blindly angered and hurt many people. I am deeply sorry. My journey was so full of many heart-pounding "UPS AND DOWNS" and countless unexpected hair-raising moments at every turn that this book cannot begin to capture them all. So, I will try my best to simplify them, in this incredible story of self-awareness. Not only for my children's sake, but also to make my theory simple enough that any child will understand it. The pain I caused them and my parents, along the way, will always haunt me. I will die with that one inescapable regret. The rest pale in comparison and yes, sadly enough, there are many more. (Read on: my story is ripe with "sex, drugs, and rock and roll." Just kidding . . . NOT!)

Inevitably, it didn't matter how bad things got, I pressed on. It was as if destiny itself had a grip on me and my fate was sealed. How could I really have free will when I chose to let the evidence rule the outcome of my search for answers? I was about to find out, as I tenaciously took on the age old question plaguing mankind and his religion: destiny vs.

free will! The really eerie thing about my story is that it all began with a somewhat fictional mysterious dream of the future I had in 1989. And, yes, much to my horror and disbelief, it was a future that reveals this answer. Naturally, I'm not going to tell you the ending. However, I will tell you that the dream tortured me mercilessly and drove me close to the brink of madness, many, many times.

I quickly "followed" this mysterious prophetic dream and found out how little I really knew about the world around me. It was weird to find that in some cultures dreams are the real world. Was my dream real? I struggled long and hard with this scenario and in the end, "SOMEHOW ALREADY KNEW" the torturous and yet beautiful truth about "US/MANKIND" that the dream had revealed. Ultimately, I would keep asking myself only two questions. Well, except for the obvious one, right. The same one I hope you are asking yourself now: "COULD MY DREAM COME TRUE?" Again, I won't tell you. The dream doesn't let me! The two ultimate questions I kept asking myself are the same ones that every mortal human asks himself in this world of death and uncertainty: "WHERE THE

HELL DID EVERYTHING COME FROM?" and "WHY DOES LIFE STAY AWAY FROM US?"

My parents' religion couldn't answer either of these questions enough to satisfy me, so I studied them all. However, it did little to answer them, too. Science finally opened my eyes and unlocked the true meaning of primitive man's universal superstitious answer/source to everything. It was universally a story of god or people/gods in "HEAVEN" that created us and everything else. This made sense, since we also are going there! They always existed, which sounded like the atom. That sounded just like the first man's name in "MY PARENTS' BIBLE." Adam. Wow! This was one of my first amazing clues to solving this mystery. Read on and you will see how it inadvertently epitomizes these two ultimate questions I just mentioned: "WHERE THE HELL DID EVERYTHING COME FROM? and WHY DOES LIFE STAY AWAY FROM US?"

Achieving scientific knowledge of these obviously similar "religious stories" has forever changed me. I quickly learned that history and religion are one and the same. And they are filled with an unimaginable horror of one conquest after another at the hands of power-hungry, inhumane leaders. Yesterday's lies became today's truths, and tomorrow is a world I would not want to be part of, if history does, in fact, repeat itself. Many times, I was more often than not apprehensive and afraid as I sorted through our world of misinformation, to arrive at the "torturous, yet wonderful truth I found about our species." But was it really our species that is wonderful? That became the scary question when I was letting the evidence rule my answer. I can't tell you any more, yet! I still don't know everything, but I do know one thing, now, for sure. I just know that I have to live in an infinite universe, where life should exist "everywhere." I just have to! Don't worry, you will find out why! Enjoy my story!

Before I continue, I want to start by saying that I am not special and only have four years of college education. Consequently, I do pursue knowledge relentlessly and have discovered that an almost incomprehensible thing has happened to me. I have developed a theory, the "THEORY OF EVERYTHING," that is brand new! It is really hard to fathom, still. But I still haven't found anyone else yet who has my solution to this theory! And amazingly enough, this would have to be true in order for the dream to be real! Could it be destiny? I can hardly believe it myself. I will tell you what it is later. I have been quoting and capitalizing words for you, as clues, to my final "ANSWER ABOUT US AND THEM." Good luck and enjoy!

Although, I'm the first to present my theory, I know that anyone could do the same and possibly solve our mystery as well. In my mind, all it took was infinite thinking. This is my greatest hope, that we will all think scientifically infinite! I hope everyone will try to think about contact with extraterrestrial life that is infinitely scientifically more advanced than us. You can start by just trying to think about our future technologies and discoveries. Please challenge me and follow the evidence only as you read my story. I found that the key to unlock our future was chiseled in stone, from the beginnings of our past to the obvious goal of our future. They all had a common bond of religious stories, with "PEOPLE IN THE SKY CREATING US TO SERVE." Wow, this sounds familiar. I began!

I studied history and ironically enough, if

this book becomes successful I want no followers, in hopes of stopping history from repeating itself. Followers create leaders and leaders create power. I don't want to be followed. We all know how power can corrupt the human mind and power has been proven to be the root of corruption from the beginning, to this very day. "WE ARE ALL WEAK TO POWER." I want to stay strong and just give. My ultimate goal is to give provable scientific hope of immortality to those seeking it. I feel that I have found it scientifically! Ultimately you will be the judge of that.

This is not about right or wrong, and please correct me if I am. I was factually wrong many times in my previous books and I could be wrong here. So please feel free to correct me "when" I'm wrong. I don't like being ignorant of anything, even though I truly understand how ignorance can be blissful, especially when it comes to the harsh reality of mankind. Besides "the theory of everything," this is also my answer to "FERMI'S PARADOX." It really is the ultimate and only question to answer, for "BELIEVERS" who think that life much further advanced than us should or does exist "EVERYWHERE" in the universe. "AND YES WE MUST ANSWER THIS FOR OUR CHILDREN'S SAKE. THEY DIDN'T ASK TO BE HERE." Here's the dreaded question: If life "SHOULD/DOES" exist, extraterrestrially or heavenly, why don't they openly live with us? "OPENLY" being the key word in life's biggest mystery, "MANKIND'S SOLIDARITY!"

This book is for all those people like myself who wake up and think, "I must be having a nightmare." I do this, because in my mind, I should live in a universe where "LIFE SHOULD EXIST EVERYWHERE IN SPACE ON SPACECRAFT" and not permanently on "PLANETS; THEY'RE LIVING HELLS." It's scary enough to "KNOW" how primitive we are now, all alone stranded on this little planet, but to look back at our "recent" past is downright, frighteningly, "LIFE CHANGING." Anyway, that's just me and I'm sure I'm not alone in trying to make sense of my existence. Fortunately, I have found ancient evidence that proves "INTELLIGENT" life is everywhere and much further advanced than us, just like I had hoped and dreamed it should be. Most importantly, they don't live on planets either. And, oh yeah, they've conquered death. That's the biggie to me; I have kids!

I recently lost my brother to a freak tragic accident and want to dedicate this book to him. He was killed by a train while trying to help me promote this book. I miss him so much and life will never be the same. Everybody loved Terry, and Terry loved everybody! Watch his movie *The Elephant in the Living Room*" (which could be a fitting title to this book and my story as well) and you will know the love that I am lucky enough to know. If only everybody could know him, the world would be a better place. He was a born optimist! Thank you so much, Terry, you helped make my life beautiful! I came home and immediately did a rewrite in his honor. I am dedicating everything to him and do believe we were destined to be together. So far, he is only one of a few that truly thinks I could have the answer to the "THE THEORY OF EVERYTHING." I am humbled by this, because he is not only scientifically intelligent, but a "FOLLOWER OF SCIENTIFIC EVIDENCE" as well! Everybody can "PROUDLY CHALLENGE" the evidence, but few can "HUMBLY FOLLOW" it! Terry is able to follow the evidence.

Finally, I truly feel I have done something "WORTHWHILE" for my two sons. They didn't deserve the death sentence that I gave them! None of us do, and Terry didn't either, but "WE ALL DIE" and we all know, that no amount of money can stop it. But do we really. Look at the progress we made last year alone in medicine and you won't be so sure. I'm an optimist and think it's "POSSIBLE TO OVERCOME DEATH." Yes, some people call me crazy; well, a lot of people do, really. But that's okay. As long as I'm crazy, I'll never really know it anyway. So, let's please give all that we can, so our "LOVE" can cure death! That's not crazy. If we can all agree that the only thing we take with us is what we give while we were here, then it's time for everyone to put their money where their mouth is and give. Wouldn't we give everything to have them back? All of us who never had a million dollars can remember as kids saying, "If I only had a million dollars" that we would help everyone. I will give all that I can to the poor and assure you that I will never have even close to a million dollars. I will limit myself to a few hundred thousand! I am asking—no, I am begging—everyone to do the same. I am doing this in honor of my brother Terry and all those whom we loved that died before him. I am lucky to have a family full of givers! Now, without any further ado, please enjoy my story and judge for yourself the validity of this amazing evidence that "LIFE EXISTS EVERYWHERE IN THE UNIVERSE." The front cover is your first clue as to why they stay away. All the words that are capitalized and quoted are clues also.

I am one of these scientific/"RELIGIOUS" people who believes life should exist everywhere. "IN THE BEGINNING" I was open to life not existing elsewhere also, but the burden of those "non-BELIEVERS" and "EVIDENCE" to prove this claim has failed to do so. "SCIENCE HAS PROVEN" that the ingredients for life are abundant throughout the universe and the fact that it is still INFINITE dictates it does exist everywhere. The infinite nature of it and the atom rules out any numerical odds of it not existing. Stephen Hawking recently stated, "The universe couldn't come from "NOTHING" or it would have nothing now." I used this same logic in questioning religion's "HEAVEN" story. Believe me, "EVEN THOUGH THEY AREN'T HERE NOW,"

I sometimes often wanted the evidence to support the "PERFECT" heaven scenario. It would have been much less "TORTUROUS" and easier to accept than having evidence of benevolent beings not "OPENLY" helping us. Unfortunately, this is what I found. It tortured me because their hiding in heaven when they can't be hurt or killed is illogical, and how could any father or person of a loving nature not stop a drunken father from sodomizing a child, if he could do so. To me "LOVE, LOGIC, and INTELLIGENCE" are the same and this is illogical. Worse yet though, is their knowing this before they created us.

Come on, people! Their "PERFECT" heaven story must be flawed. I never could buy the omnipotence of religion's god or gods, because the world isn't perfect. This is the same logic Stephen Hawking used in his deduction that the world couldn't have come from nothing! Why don't we all think this way? It's just simple common sense! Occam's Razor says the simplest answer is usually the answer. This "IS" the simple answer. I will explain more later. Now, back to my story.

Don't be surprised if you don't know what

the "Theory of Everything" is. I didn't either, until I started "SEEKING" religious and scientific answers in 1999 when I was 38 years old. It quickly became apparent to me that it is what religion was all about. Fortunately, I just didn't "INHERIT" their story. I started to look at science and it took me a long time before I even discovered it or Fermi's Paradox. Again, fortunately, both are what religion is all about. Its story supported my suspicions all along and I didn't even know it. Go figure, huh? And by the way, if you don't think I could've have solved them, then you might as well stop reading and put the book down. This is the same as looking for Jesus or an extraterrestrial and not believing anyone that says they are him. It's a universal disease I call the Jesus Paradox. You will read about my encounter with this problem later on.

Anyway, these questions became a constant nagging conundrum I had to solve, not only for me but for my two sons. I brought them into a world of uncertainty, except for one thing, a death sentence. How could I have done this! Now, guilt and mental anguish over this selfless act alone drives me more than anything else. Before "I WOKE UP" to this reality, I was really just doing it for myself and the sheer exciting challenge of doing what "no other had done." Well, allegedly hadn't done. The whole "CIVILIZED" world knows the Jesus story.

But was this real history or not? I had to see for myself if it was fact or fiction. I was determined that even if it turns out to be real, the fact that he isn't "OPENLY" here now would still make me challenge it. Especially, the omnipotence factor, because bad stuff happened then and still does now, everywhere! Come on, who wouldn't make the world perfect for their kids? They would for us! After I had my mental awakening, I must admit to becoming obsessed with being the first to do so, as my story will vividly show. I had to do it for my kids. I couldn't stand the thought of them dying!

The first thing I did was to start researching the archaeological record of early man. The Jesus story was "ROCK" solid in history. I couldn't dispute it. As a matter of fact, very few people contested his existence, because of the overwhelming historical proof. He became the most famous man in the world, because he said he was God and predicted his death for doing so. More astonishingly he predicted his resurrection (coming back to life), as well. This was not only incredible, but it is just what I felt would be scientifically possible by extraterrestrials more advanced than us. I could hardly believe it; I had found proof of what I was looking for. Conquering death wasn't an imaginary possibility; it was real history, and now maybe even our future. No, according to him, my mind and science future it is real! I just had to prove it, "LIKE A LAWYER." I had the toughest case of all. A murder without a body.

Jesus said he was a Jew, which was a priesthood of the Sumerians. Wow, unbelievably enough, they came from our oldest written records! I was blown by this necessary and fundamental evidence; it wouldn't have fit in any other way. Moreover, these records led to finding plenty of ancient clay tablets claiming the existence of heavenly or extraterrestrial beings with primitive man. The tablets depicted them as "GIANTS." This puzzled me and led me to pursue their "REAL DIFFERENCE IN APPEARANCE." "THIS BECAME OBVIOUS AS I LOOKED AT OTHER CULTURES." I was even more blown away that there are even two intertwined snakes involved in our creation story, like the two trees in the Garden of Eden. They look just like DNA! No way. This is how we create new species today that wouldn't otherwise evolve. How could this be, unless they are real scientists, just like us? What's even more astounding is the fact that it became the AMA symbol we know today!

But, what really shocked me the most were the universal "ANCIENT" depictions of flying saucers and an alien-looking being, with a big bald head! I found them on every continent and in every ancient culture all over the earth! Later, I "SAW" that the universal halo symbol, "THE ONE MADE FAMOUS BY THE JUDEO-CHRISTIAN STORY," could be their flying saucer. Then, I discovered that it too was everywhere! Obviously the Sumerians, like all the others, forgot what the god/gods/angels looked like. It must've become the universal symbol to distinguish them from man and connect them to heaven, which was universally the sky. It seemed so obvious to me. I began to research this period of history as much as I could. Aha! This is when something went wrong and our mystery started. I found that this period is called the "GOLDEN AGE" and preceded our current history of "ONLY" six thousand years. After they made man to serve him/them the angels/gods started mating with them. However, "THEY WEREN'T SUPPOSED TO." This was what started our mystery; the key was in the giant story! The "CERNES GIANT" on the front cover represents this era. Could these aliens be these heavenly beings? Could the body of the Cernes Giant represent the same mixture as a mother goddess statue, I found by the Sumerians. Both heads looks like an alien. I was on to something "BIG."

I found that the Cernes Giant even has an ancient saucer above his head (shown just in illustrations), which matches some of today's famous sightings and my own. And yes, believe it or not, I finally found and filmed a flying saucer. I STILL FILM THEM TODAY! You will see them along with many others in the illustrations following this letter. Yes, this is also a letter to my children, as well as all the children of the world. Filming flying saucers is undoubtedly the most important discovery I've made along the way. Because, there is also no truer saying than "SEEING IS BELIEVING!" And believe me, kids will believe it when it happens to them as well! Kids will not doubt their existence ever again, because we teach them that the evidence/facts rule. Whatever anyone else "BELIEVES" is "UP" to them. I did find out much more than I bargained for about this giant statue. "COINCIDENTLY" it was something I knew all along and "SOMETHING KIDS EVEN KNOW." Read on, please!

The following years would fly by as I began furiously writing my books. My mind was filled with many more exciting and profound discoveries that would change my life forever. Except for seeing and filming my flying saucer, which didn't happen until much later, nothing compared to the scientific epiphany I had in "DISCOVERING HEAVEN'S LOCATION." The ancient stories "MATCHED" today's science. Didn't everyone know space is "UP" and is heaven to us, as well? This proves heaven is space and "NOT A DIMENSION, SPIRIT WORLD, OR FRAME OF MIND." I was literally floored to find it being supported, not only by all ancient stories, but with ancient rock art as well. We could trust this evidence, like matching fingerprints today. The evidence is "ROCK SOLID." This was amazing! "UP" alone became and still is the most simple crucial scientific evidence that hit me like a ton of bricks in solving our mystery. We now live up in the sky, too! These heavenly beings have to be real and not spirit. This should be a no-brainer for everyone, huh? Read on, because it isn't and the findings of my search may shock you. It did me.

The ancient artworks all over the earth come from a "SIMPLE" common source, beings "UP" in the sky. I even found that the Mayans painted their gods blue because they were also depicted as men. The painting helped the natives to distinguish them as gods. The reason was obvious to them, because they all knew heaven was the sky! "THEY ALL KNEW THEIR GODS LIVED IN THE SKY." They just didn't know what they looked like. I was fast closing in on what I had been "UNKNOWINGLY" looking for all along. What they looked like. The craziest part of this finding is that my parents, like almost every religious person I've encountered, don't think that heaven is really the sky. To them and almost everyone else it's a spirit world, dimension, or frame of mind. Yet, they look "UP" to this day and then bow "DOWN" their heads to pray! The ancients knew it, but we don't. I could understand them giving up their spirit story, because they didn't fly. But we do, so let's get over it! If they saw and made a statue of their god's rocket, plane, or saucer, then it is what they will return in! We shouldn't tickle children's ears with "freedom of speech" anymore when it comes to knowledge, whether it be the past or present. Facts are facts and I'm sorry if it makes their parents, or anybody else, for that matter, look bad. Thank god "UP" is chiseled in stone and throughout history. At least, we have one case of brain-washing that isn't all bad. As a matter of fact, it is crucial to understanding my "THEORY OF EVERYTHING."

I thought this discovery would gain world-wide recognition in my third book, *The Future Alien Contact* and fourth book *2012, Gold's History Solves Mankind's Mystery*. I had many depictions epitomizing this ancient "UP" evidence. More importantly, I had a picture of Johnny Cash looking "UP" at a flying saucer! It was huge to me, since Johnny is world-wide famous and his saucer matched an ancient 17,000-year-old cave drawing of one! That would do it, I thought. It didn't. Oddly enough, I became partners with a UFO hunter who recently filmed one identical to the one Johnny filmed, 20 years earlier. I thought this would be equivalent to digging one up! It wasn't. Nothing worked, but I didn't stop there, either!

Furthermore, I pointed out the amazing coincidental matching evidence that space exploration is only made possible with gold, and our history is rooted in gold mining! It was even the universal sacred offering for these gods in the sky. I gave them one example after another, but nothing worked. Not even my halo/saucer connection coupled with the fact, that "WE ALSO USE GOLD TO MAKE OUR SPACECRAFT." I could not understand how they "DIDN'T SEE" that their god's fiery chariot/spacecraft "COULD POSSIBLY BE THESE FLYING SAUCERS MADE OF GOLD." (But I would soon "SEE" how and why.)

Therefore, on my fifth book, I put a statue of Easter Island "LOOKING UP." It has an "alleged" hat, along with my partner's flying saucer video shot above it! They matched. WOW! This proved to me that they were looking for their god/gods to return in flying saucers! Again, "TO ME" this was amazing matching evidence that spoke volumes! I even named my book after this amazing discovery, because of a Barbara Walters' special, where she asked a panel of "EXPERTS" the location of heaven. I couldn't believe it, but no one said space like me! This was mind-boggling. Was I the only one getting this science future reality? They all thought it was a dimensional world, frame of mind, or "SPIRIT" world, just like my parents. I simply titled my book *Heaven Is Space … Up"* because that's what the statue was doing, looking up to heaven! Simple enough, right? Well, guess again, because it still didn't get any attention. I was shocked and dumbfounded. I actually found out where heaven was and nobody cared or believed me! Even worse, they usually got angry about it! What? No way. How could this happen? Well, I guess it's because I found out that everybody wants to go to heaven, but just not right now. LOL!

How could people change heaven's location "IN THEIR MIND" when the evidence hasn't changed. How could they not see the contradiction in looking up and then saying, It is a spirit world, frame of mind, or dimension? I knew how. I stated this fact on the opening page of the fifth book. (The evidence didn't change—the people's story did!) This evidence solved the "ALLEGED HAT" mystery, for me. I thought it would do it for everyone. It didn't, and needless to say, hardly anyone took me seriously about this being the craft that they will return in. At the very least, though, I thought it would clearly explain where heaven is, like the title stated.

Well, I was wrong. I took it to ABC and tried to give it to Barbara. They said they would, but as you well know by reading this, that it "APPARENTLY" didn't affect them or her either, if she got it. Lucky for me "UP" was already chiseled in stone throughout our history. "THANK GOD" we all still look up. LOL. They can't deny that evidence, no matter where they say it is! I've even started asking religious people everywhere where it is. "THEY ALL SAY THE SAME THREE ANSWERS THAT BARBARA'S PANEL DID." Then I tricked them into looking up. But, it didn't work either; it just made them mad!

Now, back to my story. It's obvious, with all this evidence, that these gods/god/angels must have conquered space! They had to be real flesh and blood beings like us. This would explain how they could scientifically create a new self-destructive species like us and it solves the missing-link problem! This is the simple answer. People, we need to go "UP" ourselves!

Besides this amazing discovery (which is the title of my sixth book, *The Discovery*) I've found many statues of spacecraft identical to the ones that we have today! We even have a Sumerian clay tablet showing our solar system in its exact order, size, and distance, that we have only proven in the last 50 years! We now acknowledge a tenth planet that they said existed then! The Jewish Bible, like all religious texts, gives us plenty of examples, pointing toward the angels and gods being flesh and blood beings. The most famous is made famous in the Flood story. Their God condemned this mixing and killed everyone on earth except for Noah, including "INNOCENT CHILDREN." Read on, please. Everybody loves a good mystery, and I promise you this is a humdinger.

I feverishly continued to research our human fossil record looking for any statues of aliens, and found an abundance of them. I not only found them in the Sumerian culture but everywhere, from the heads of Easter Island to the head molding of the Egyptians and Peruvians! This begged me to look even further at our fossil record. So I did, and when I looked at the missing link evidence, something stood out like a flashing neon sign. There was a distinct missing period of skull growth about 200,000 years ago. Modern man came on the scene with an upright, overly large bulbous head. The aliens must've been mixing with them!

Wow, maybe the aliens are real, after all. I found plenty of artwork from about 50,000 years ago resembling aliens to a T. However, as time went on the artworks of these gods/angels/god started to be men with wings instead. It seemed apparent that after they left, men only knew where they were, as represented by the wings, and began to forget what they looked like. The last Ice Age was about 13,000 years ago, which coincidentally created a global flood. What an incredible coincidence . . . or is it? We are missing history and it could be on our coastlines, submerged just out of sight. We are only now discovering these ancient settlements.

This evidence proves the alien/flying saucer phenomenon didn't begin with Hollywood, like some anti-UFO religious people said it did. Religion was already demonizing this evidence, only because they can't explain it away. They couldn't because we have presidents, astronauts and even children seeing them. This was a no-brainer. I knew these people would say or do anything to defend their "BELIEFS." I could understand it from them. But from my family, this I didn't understand.

I "innocently" ridiculed their powerful Hollywood devil story. How could they be so logical and scientific one minute and then totally illogical the next. Do they really believe "HE'S" going to remain invisible in a world of people who would follow him for money in a NEW YORK minute. It's a bad religious joke! Come on, we have video cams today. I am filming flying saucers; why can't they film something from the devil? My family and religion would surprise me. I never had a clue how powerful religion really was and is, until this happened. I find it hard to understand why it still is divided today, when it's all about being back "UP" with the good guys. Crazy, huh? I started with religion because "MY PARENTS BIBLE" basically said the same thing science says about life in the universe. Heavenly beings should exist "UP" in the sky, "OMNIPRESENTLY." This "HUGE MATCHING" fact alone, kept me looking for more evidence of contact with primitive man by an extraterrestrial or these heavenly beings. I thought it was big!

Even though I have written six books since I began this harrowing journey in 1999, I have sold very few. Ironically enough, the title to my first book is named after a Revelation Bible prophecy that isn't received well either. Stands to reason why I haven't sold many, huh? Especially if the well-known biblical quote about people finding heaven is true; "FEW WILL ENTER." Not surprisingly, it is because they don't "BELIEVE." Wow, this became my struggle. Don't worry, that's why I eventually titled a book after the 2012 prophecy, so I'd still have a shot. LOL! Now, back to the beginning. It's crucial to understand why I became so obsessed with solving our mystery. Too many things were falling into place. I was beginning to think that destiny could, in fact, be real. Is it possible that no one else was seeing this?

My first book is called *The Two Witnesses and the Religion Cover-up* and oddly enough mirrored my dilemma. At the end, the witnesses get killed for their prophecy, but are resurrected! This tugged at me and intrigued me at the same time, for two reasons. First, they must've had an answer to "THE THEORY OF EVERYTHING" that bothered everyone. Because in spite of the prophecy's "terrible message" it was accepted world-wide; the two witnesses tortured the WORLD with their prophecy. Secondly, this sounded like the same struggle I see today, with science fighting ancient religion's "TRADITIONAL" strongholds. There are many cases in the past verifying the possibility of science defeating an ancient religious tradition. The Romans thought the world was flat and yet they looked at round celestial bodies day and night! This intrigued me immensely. I would ask myself how this could be, but I already know. Could their prophecy be a scientific one, with future implications that will adversely affect all humanity, especially religion?

I was shocked that this is the point of solving of time's enigma, as the Scripture states, "TIME WILL BE NO MORE" and another "FINAL

RESURRECTION." This was the point of contact with these beings "UP" in the sky. Wow, this was logical to happen at this point. Maybe they cracked what Albert Einstein was trying so desperately to do: create a unified field theory! How is this possible? This was truly mind-boggling. Again, how could we find evidence of future sciences that we haven't achieved ourselves, without accepting the fact that destiny could be real. The future of mankind's conquering space could have happened with another species. They could have created us and be controlling our isolation from them. They must be benevolent, but unable to live with us. I found that the Scripture where mankind is called the number 666 ("That which isn't, was and will be . . .") not only indicates time has been solved, but also that mankind is a scientific creation that would never evolve and his species is incurable as a whole. WOW! WOW! WOW!

Even more importantly, though, with their prophecy the mystery of "GOD" was finished! This was what I was looking for: a resurrection that doesn't allow our mystery to continue. "Thank god."(You see, I'm guilty too, just like the Romans' flat-world conditioned response.) I learned how to use a concordance. I had wanted to cut through the chase and went right to the word *mystery*! I couldn't believe my "LUCK." I couldn't help but tingle all over with excitement at the possibility of doing this. Why didn't I do this in the beginning? Little did I know how much I was about to learn. Could I be one of them? My first book still rivets me when I read it. I did make contact with something!

I became entranced with religion because it described a future I felt is scientifically possible, except for the omnipotence. It describes where we are going and what life should be like for us in space. Man, did it ever seem *Star Trek*-ish to me and I loved *Star Trek*! Wow, funny how I didn't realize the importance of the name, *star*. The pursuit of future earths is only made possible with stars! They are suns! And I never understood why god only had "SONS/SUNS." If god is invisible and everything, then this makes perfect scientific sense of religion's invisible omnipresent god story and sending his son as himself. We are all suns/sons, because they are made of atoms! Check out the back cover again and read on!

The coincidences get better with religion matching and describing science realities. I'll think twice before I ever discount the old adage "WHAT'S IN A NAME" again, believe me. Please remember this clue to solving our mystery! I have been giving you clues with all the quoted capitalized words, but this is the most important. You will find out why at the end. I will tell you the answer to who we are and where we came from with one word! Now back to my story.

It's painfully obvious, that these beings aren't openly existing with us and yet we seem to be fulfilling their inevitable predestined story. Could the inevitable be "SCIENTIFIC KNOWLEDGE" as the Bible predicts, "a spreading of knowledge all over the earth"? Science seems to be doing this very thing, and it definitely is unstoppable! Could this inevitable knowledge be a torturous truth about our species that we will not like? Are these beings, real flesh-and-blood "SPACE DWELLERS" who have already done what we are about to do ?

After all, they universally live "UP" in the heaven/sky, like our scientific future is obviously "DESTINED" for. We all know from Captain Kirk that "SPACE IS OUR FINAL FRONTIER"!

This became the haunting question I set out to prove. "WHO ARE THESE BEINGS AND WHAT DO THEY LOOK LIKE?" I was about to find an unbelievably "IRREFUTABLE CORRELATION" between their power struggle, which caused a separation and our own struggle for power, which keeps us separated. Ultimately, "THEIR LUST FOR POWER" led to their "DOWNFALL." The losers are thrown down to earth, in hell! I couldn't believe it! Religion described the structure of life in the universe as we know it. Mother Nature makes this hell. We could easily conquer space and keep our enemies on a planet, stripped of "KNOWLEDGE" and then heaven would be up to us and them, as well. Wow! I can't believe this matches. But we're the lucky ones because they supposedly save us, or do they? "WHO SAVED THEM" since it already happened to them? (This is a clue.)

Ultimately, where they came from was what I was looking for. If I found this out, it should lead me to the answer of "WHERE DID EVERYTHING COME FROM?" Little did I know, what I was about to discover would change my reality forever. I discovered what they truly "LOOKED" like. They all looked the same! This was astonishingly simple proof to me that they came from natural evolutionary processes, like "ALL NATURE'S CREATIONS, WHICH LOOK THE SAME." All I had to do was look around me. Every species but us multiplies like they were stamped out of a printing press. We're the only thing different and it gives us power over one another! This was simple enough that "CHILDREN WILL SEE IT." I was so happy. This is "WHAT I TRULY HOPED FOR ALL ALONG."

The outcome of my findings definitely tortured the majority of people around me, and for that I am sorry. Many times it tortured me as well. I will tell you, though, that I was born an optimist and will die one, and yes, my final answer is optimistic! I will tell you that much. As a matter of fact, I still get a kick out of my third book's warning on the bottom cover: "The future looks bright so wear cheap sunglasses." It was at least better than my first, which said: "Warning: This book may be harmful to your health"! Now, I know the true meaning of "BE CAREFUL WHAT YOU WISH FOR." It is blatantly obvious with the title and warning to my second book: *Aliens Gold Tenth Planet* and the warning, "This book may be HARMFUL TO YOUR WEALTH." Religion is anti-wealth.

I am finishing with this final book in hopes of easing my children's fear of death. I am eaten up with the idea of conquering death! Could they really have made this a reality? It is logical, if they conquered space like their story says they did. The universal religious story of creating humans is, as well. My mind now stayed full of futuristic visions I had since only dreamed of. Was my dream coming true? Believe it or not, I was scared of this possibility. I'm not as strong as I want to be and still fear death. Not as the end, but an awakening to the universal religious theme and logical future scientific possibility that "Nothing is hidden that won't be revealed" being scientifically possible. Wouldn't this be a wonderful reality for children facing a perverted sexual adult, but a nightmare for adults who have been evil? The evidence you are about to see not only confirms this scenario, but also scientifically conquering immortality itself. Please open your mind to what we could achieve one thousand years from now and trust me, this doesn't seem too far-fetched. Entertain the idea that life exist infinitely and conquering death is a given!

Now, you "MIGHT" be thinking— and I can't say as I blame you for doing so—that I'm probably just another arrogant, egotistical, self-proclaimed guru wanting to be "FOLLOWED." Well, I'm not and I don't! I not only want you to challenge me, but I hope you do the same to everyone and even more importantly, yourself. Any good crime detective would do the same. I finally did. I became a detective, because my parents' "GOD" supposedly created us and this chaotic hellish species called "MANKIND." I asked them why, when he could've made it perfect "IF HE WANTED TO." They really didn't know and always gave me the original sin story of why we aren't perfect now. Then they gave me the universal answer, when I said it was ridiculous, "THAT GOD WORKS IN MYSTERIOUS WAYS." But why couldn't they explain Mother Nature. This really bothered me, as well as "HIM" wanting to be worshipped. This is a disease in today's world where we are militarily trying to enforce equality. Crazy, huh, having to force equality? However, their god's addiction to power and our own would help me to eventually solve this mystery.

My parents also couldn't explain "SENSIBLY" why he stays hidden from us, either. I told them that he sounded like a criminal who premeditated the crime and his getaway. They don't care for their victims! And sure enough, I read that very thing in the beginning of the Bible: "God repented the day he made man." What? No way! He knew he was doing something bad before he did it? I had to figure this out. This was illogical, people, and it happened only six thousand years ago. That's only sixty one-hundred-year periods, or sixty great-grandpas! How could history get so screwed up, in such a short period of time? For god's sake, I was a history major in college. I knew I could solve this. I know history is religion. They're all founded upon it; they are one and the same! The earth appeared to be a crime scene according to universal religion and their creator was "CLEARLY" gone.

Little did I know back then that I was about to embark on a journey of discovery that would change my life forever. Never, in my wildest dreams, did I imagine solving what Mom and Dad couldn't. And unknowingly to them, I never would have done it without their help. They "INNOCENTLY SUBJECTED ME TO RELIGION", not science. But much to my surprise, these two fields agreed in the most fundamental concept of life, that life exist elsewhere in the universe. More importantly, they both agree that it is "UP",in the sky. People, couldn't real flesh and blood beings have conquered space, created humans for "BEAUTY/ POWER" and gotten addicted to our unstoppable "REALITY"? If so, do they look like us? This question became the driving force behind solving our mystery. It literally blew me away. Why didn't anybody else see this possibility?

I was about to bust my bubble. I soon discovered that author Erich von Daniken did. Although his theory and mine differ in two ways. The first I will explain now; the second will be explained at the end. It will shed light on the importance of the most famous man's name and our addiction to power through beauty of the flesh. Erich became famous with his book *Chariot of the Gods* and has now been dubbed the founder of the ancient astronaut theory. I immediately saw his term "ancient" astronaut as a stumbling block for thinking infinitely. I felt lucky, because Captain Kirk and Jesus both described the universe to a T, like me; "Space is the final frontier" and "Heaven is our our throne, the earth a footstool." Wow! Again, this realization blew me away. This infinite thinking is only now universal knowledge, and it's 2011. Or at least I thought so; the reality is scary. They don't see planets as dangerous! Most don't think infinitely! How could this be? I would soon "CLEARLY" see how.

WOW, Jesus must've been and is an "INFINITE ASTRONAUT" like Kirk! They don't live on planets but see them as paradises to temporarily rest on. We all should know that earths are living hells at the expense of Mother Nature. The evidence is all around us on a daily basis. Surely we all know this, but I found most religious people don't. My parents have fallen prey to the paradise earth story. I understand why, because their religion paints a beautiful Hollywood picture of god's omnipotence, to make it so. I hope it is possible, as I also love the earth's beauty. But as beautiful as it is, it is full of natural catastrophes! That's why it should be just a resting spot! We should all scientifically "SEE" that space is the only place where we can assure our immortality and control our destiny.

Anyway, this infinite astronaut possibility consumed me. I always felt life should exist everywhere in the universe because it does here. I tried hard, but just couldn't find the evidence to buy my parents superstitious omnipotent spirit god source. Let alone that "HE" always existed. Unless "HE" is the atom as the back cover suggests. This evidence explained the hell all around us. It is easy to see how advanced space dwellers' contact with primitive man would've created all the magical spirit traditions. Everything we've discovered in the universe is "PHYSICAL" and not "SPIRIT." It is made of atom/energy and is very real. Surprisingly, it also has no beginning and ending like their god and is invisible (to the naked eye), too. Again, these two very scientific and religious facts agree! What? No way!

I really felt I was on to something here. Something big, like proof of everything always existing! How can this be? Well, we all know that matter just "CHANGES FORM." I used water as an example for children. I saw how this clearly highlighted the confusion of Christianity. Is god a man or spirit? I even found that Christianity is really just divided into two thoughts, one believing god is Jesus and the other that Jesus is the son of god. It all stemmed from this simple lack of knowledge about matter. The trinity concept in religion is really simple physics; everything is made of solid, liquid or gas atoms/Adams! Read on, PLEASE!

Religion isn't the only field that seems immune to logic when it comes to the universe. How can scientist keep saying the universe is huge, or using distance, to explain the reasoning for extraterrestrial life not contacting us? Even worse, why would they indicate life exists on other planets, if it is more advanced than us? They obviously aren't thinking infinitely! Why don't they see that religion is describing Michio Kaku's stage-three civilization? I really felt that the key to solving our mystery is infinite thinking. No, I'm sure of it. I was onto something with my new "INFINITE ASTRONAUT THEORY." Something that now could actually be proven with hard scientific evidence and history. I relentlessly followed this matching evidence in hopes of solving these two questions about life.

I wanted to do it for my children as I'm sure any parent would, like mine tried. I don't begrudge them for resorting to religion in explaining where everything came from. It was what their parents did to them. It was "TRADITION." Heck, most of the world does it that way. So, why I was different? I guess it's because of the rebellious times I was born in, the 1960s. I definitely wasn't a follower and became more determined than ever to prove things to myself.

Was destiny true? Could I be one of these two witnesses? I pressed on, but I didn't "PROVE IT" to myself. I shared "MY EVIDENCE" with everyone. Or better yet, I should say, harassed/tortured everyone. That is what truly happened and it was a mistake I will always deeply regret. You will find out why as you read my entire story. I became what I was running from, an evidence zealot. I soon found that seeking itself can become the disease. "IT" made me want to know everything! Now, back to my story.

This "Theory of Everything" that I so obsessively pursued is really better summed up by children asking, "Where did everything come from?"

To me, this became a silly question, since I've learned everything is made of atoms and they can't be created or destroyed. We have the answer already, and yet the majority of the adult world is either ignorant of it or doesn't see it. I didn't. Either way, I found that children quickly "SEE" this contradiction between religion's creation and science's evolution. Especially if you point it out to them. Fortunately, religious tradition hasn't completely brainwashed them, yet. I typed with passion!

Suddenly and much to my surprise, my niece Madyson interrupted me, very condescending-like, "You do know that there aren't any silly questions, don't you?" She must've been reading over my shoulder. I immediately chuckled and agreed with her. I really got a kick out of her sudden teacher-like behavior. She wasn't about to let me off easy for anything and wanted to make sure that I knew she was smart, too. I had been songwriting with her earlier. "SHE WANTS TO BE FAMOUS" just like Miley Cyrus! She is my brother-in-law's little girl and was in for the weekend. But, try as she might, she couldn't understand how this could be. She wanted desperately to know more.

"How could everything always exist?" she questioned me. I quickly asked her why, not wanting to lose this "GOLDEN" opportunity to talk with her alone. "Because," she said boldly, "god created everything." I suddenly had an "AIR-head" idea!

"Well," I asked immediately, "where did god come from, or better yet where is he, and why isn't he a girl, like you?" She looked puzzled and said god was invisible and everywhere. I knew she wasn't about to touch the gender thing; that was asking way too much. As smart as she was, I'm sure she had already asked Mommy that, but probably got the old "some things we can never know" answer.

"Huh," I replied. "God sounds. Just like the atom, huh. And what is the first man's name in the Bible, Madyson?"

"Adam," she quickly responded. "Wow, they match too, huh?"

"Yes they do, baby girl," I came back lovingly. "Just like the atom, huh," I replied.

"Yeah!" she said, real surprised-like. I quickly showed her the Jewish star matching the atom and explained how I was using it on the back cover of my book. I went on to explain how it will force religious people to reconcile their knowledge of religion's god and science's atom, because they contradict each other. God can't create the atom according to science! Above it, I have the very question that we were discussing: "HOW CAN THIS BE?"

"Well, ALL I KNOW IS WHAT MOMMY TAUGHT ME, and that is god created everything."

"Well, baby girl, do you know where "INVISIBLE" air comes from or goes to?" I asked her gingerly. She just shrugged her shoulders. Eureka, I discovered, that her beautiful, childlike innocence was just what I was looking for. I was writing this final letter to my children, but now I know it must be for all the children of the world. I confess to selfish reasons. I "UNKNOWINGLY" gave mine a death sentence when I brought them into the world, like all young parents do. Even worse, I constantly subjected them to their death sentence in the name of religion. It doesn't matter that I was trying to give them "HOPE." I still "SCARED THEM TO DEATH." Now, I just want to "LOVE THEM TO LIFE!" I OWE MY SONS THAT MUCH, FOR ALL THE PAIN AND FEAR I'VE "INNOCENTLY" CAUSED THEM!

Innocent or not, and it was without intent to scare them, I finally discovered Occam's Razor. It became my simple childhood rule in solving this mystery. IT IS A SCIENTIFIC RULE LIKE FERMI'S PARADOX AND NAMED AFTER A SCIENTIST who said the simplest answer is usually the correct answer. I liked this rule, because if I couldn't explain my answers to her and them, then I would fail anyway. All of a sudden, this bubbly ten-year-old began asking me what I was writing about. She unknowingly gave me the perfect setting for this ending.

I told her all about my discovery and began sharing my theory. I loved teaching kids. It's easy for us adults to see that they certainly are the only hope our future holds. We all know the old saying, "You can't teach an old dog new tricks." I found it to be especially true when it comes to religion, and oh yeah, of course politics! These are also one and the same. But you can teach kids, if their parents aren't around and it isn't too late. I didn't think it was too late with Madyson; her dad wasn't religious, only her mom, and she wasn't around! I told her my theory is so simple a child could understand by simply knowing the definition of the atom. She really didn't understand how it answered the "theory of everything" until I started to explain what it was. She stopped me and then I remembered, she had been reading over my shoulder. Duh! Well, of course I stopped telling her and grabbed the dictionary, to let her "SEE THE DEFINITION HERSELF." I wanted her to know how to check facts on her own.

Just as I started to read it, she anxiously chimed in before I could finish, "Atoms can't be created nor destroyed and they make up everything." She got so excited that I just about fell over laughing. In all the mayhem, she forgot about not knowing the answer to my "SILLY" question and I really do think she was just about to get it. Suddenly, it dawned on her and she gave me that funny look again. I knew the light bulb in her head hadn't come on completely yet and told her so. She just rolled laughing and started begging me for the answer. I told her I would first explain why this contradiction exists, because "you already said the answer, remember, silly," I said as I ribbed her. "Atoms make up everything."

She quickly squirmed to get away, but

immediately asked how this could be? I started explaining. "The contradiction exists because of religion and its primitive superstitious approach to teaching it. They teach you that God created everything and yet science teaches the opposite! The superstition is all about what God is. I spoke softly and slowly towards the end. I wanted her to understand the big words. Before I could even ask her if she understood them, she beat me to the punch and told me she knew what superstitious meant. Wow, had she read my mind? I was truly amazed at her quick-wittedness.

"I didn't mean anything by that," I said, quickly apologizing.

"I know, silly," she said sternly. "Remember, there isn't any such thing as a silly question, even dummies know that." I darn near fell out of my chair again, laughing.

"Yes, Madyson, I do know that," I answered back fondly. "Well, furthermore," I continued, "we should not only question all ancient religious stories of an omnipotent being creating the universe, but science and its Big Bang theory as well. Because, unlike the atom or god, they both have a beginning and this doesn't agree with their definition; they can't be created nor destroyed. "Matter is made of solids, liquids, and gases, baby girl, and that's everything, right?"

"Duh," she mocked me back! I loved her feistiness!

"Heck, Madyson," I laughed. "What I really always wanted to know is, what was around god or the atom, especially since they were the only thing that existed in the "Beginning." I mocked with quote gestures. She laughed also and acted like she got that, too! And maybe she did, but I kept my laughter to myself this time, not wanting to risk offending her. That was asking a little too much. Anyway, I continued to tell her she could find the answers where I had to look, in the deep theory section of *Physics for Dummies*. "I had to go there to get it, because I was a dummy, not you, Madyson." I remarked quickly as I grabbed and hugged her.

All of a sudden, she blurted that the answer to my silly question is that everything didn't come from anywhere, because it can't be created or destroyed, just like god.

"He's invisible and makes everything, too!"

She was literally jumping with enthusiasm.

"Congratulations, my little precious niece. You may have had your first eureka moment in life, just like I did. You just matched ancient religious evidence to a scientific one. I did the same thing with the symbols, remember. I'll show you more after I finish." She quickly asked me what *eureka* meant. "Eureka, meaning the light bulb going off in your head. It's what happens when you discover something big that was always there but you just didn't see it!"

"I did, didn't I?" she belted out prancing around me grinning like a Cheshire cat.

"Yes you did and I'm PROUD of you," I said as I grabbed and hugged her. "Well okay, actually, baby girl, we ought to look it up. Do you want to or do you want me to finish my story?"

"Just tell me your story," she snapped. "I want to get back to songwriting."

"Okay, I'm going to tell you my theory now, Madyson, because you are ready." She listened intently and hung onto my every word. I looked deeply into those big beautiful brown innocent eyes and began.

"My theory is an "INFINITE ASTRONAUT" one, like the definition of the atom itself. You see, Madyson, I don't think the atom's definition, matching the first man's name in the Bible, is a coincidence. Especially, when it answers the question we all want to know, 'IS THERE LIFE AFTER DEATH?' The atom says life never stops existing and if an intelligent species can survive to conquer space, then surely they could conquer immortalizing themselves. The Bible story is proof of life after death and that's what the atom proves."

She got so excited! "And guess what, baby girl, we've only recently discovered what the ancients knew and couldn't even see thousands of years ago! We now see it with an electron microscope. I also found that the Egyptian's god name is Atum, as well." She really got excited about that, too! I continued before she could break in. I wanted to get this done and get back to work.

"And now, the greatest scientific minds today theorize an infinite repeating cycle of life in the universe, like the definition of the atom! Madyson, please don't share this with your mother, at least not yet. She might get offended. You see, Madyson,

I am not allegiant to creation stories by religion's omnipotent magic god, because I detest religion's self-righteousness. This offended my parents. I didn't mean to offend them. However, I am doing this because they scared me to death, with their devil story and always reminded me I am dying. I don't want to die, baby girl, and darn sure don't want to see you or my kids die."

"Me either," she cried out. I grabbed her and hugged her.

"Well, that's why I've done all this, baby girl. I saw good matching evidence of heaven's "UP" direction/location as proof that real flesh-and-blood advanced space dwellers could have created religion. And if that's the case, then maybe they conquered death like it says. Heck, I began to ask myself simple questions like, 'Why would spirits live in the sky, how do they live and do they make babies?'" She busted out laughing, like any eleven-year-old would.

"I've grown up, Madyson, and certainly don't 'BELIEVE' in Santa Claus anymore. He's just like god, too. He's an old man with long white hair and beard. He knows if we're good or bad, too."

"Wow," she remarked excitedly. "It is just like the god story, huh?" She seemed as amazed as I did when I first realized the similarities between the two.

"Yeah, they do and, as a matter of fact," I continued, "they're living or flying through the sky matches our reality today. We also fly and live UP IN THE SKY."

Her eyes got big as saucers and she said, "Yeah, we do, huh." Then she asked weakly, "Is that why you think they do too?"

"The evidence says so," I said boldly, and that's what matters. I find it's better not to think or believe, baby girl; just follow the evidence. That's really knowing the truth of history or any mystery. Knowledge is power, baby girl, we all 'KNOW' that, right?"

She just beamed as she smiled and nodded her head yes.

"I'm going to be a scientist," she said emphatically. "And maybe I will get to bring back Wrinkles one day!" I hugged her and told her that she would make a fine scientist and if religion conquered death, then she will too and we will all see Wrinkles again! (Wrinkles was her favorite pet.)

"I have to tell you, though," I remarked further, "that I think the flying saucers I film could be them. It makes more sense than angels with wings being spirits. That would explain why primitive man gave them wings, because they knew they lived in the sky. However, I could be wrong and will follow the evidence, no matter where it ends. If I couldn't do that, I wouldn't be TRULY seeking answers. You see, Madyson, this really is all about who or what god is and most importantly where he, she or it is." (I didn't want to scare her with the possibility of what they look like.) "I don't have a problem with god or gods existing, just his or their ability to make the world perfect and not doing it! That's not logical, is it, baby girl? Wouldn't you if you could?" I asked, pleading-like.

"YES," she said resoundingly!

"WELL, ME TOO!" I responded immediately. So, since it isn't, we have to grow up and answer that question: 'Why doesn't HE/SHE/or IT?'" I asked, pointing up. We both just laughed. "I don't have a problem if he can't, baby, because you are going to do that, you little scientist you, I love you so much," I said as I hugged her again.

I continued. "The scientific/religious evidence and logic support life's existence everywhere. The problem is getting adults to rewrite the traditional universal religious stories, using today's science words. Adults refuse to do it, because they are brainwashed by their allegiance to religious tradition." I saw her bristle, just like adults, at the mention of the "B" word. So, I quickly showed her proof and said it was okay because it isn't a child's fault, nor the parents' either, to be religiously brainwashed. It's simply tradition! "You see, religious followers say that god isn't a magic Santa Claus, yet he shares the same characteristics," I replied, with one example after another. She was amazed at the similarities. But she weakly said, as if she wasn't sure of herself, "that god wasn't magic."

"Why isn't he?" I asked. She just shrugged her shoulders.

I asked her, "What do you call a man producing something from nothing?"

She said "Magic.'

"Well then," I asked delicately, "how did god do it?"

She started to reply, but just stopped. "It's the

same thing, isn't it?" She said she didn't know. I then asked her why she believed in God since she couldn't see him. "Do you think it's maybe because your mom does."

"I guess," she answered weakly.

"That's why I did, baby girl, and it's okay. It's just tradition and we all fall prey to it. However, the "JESUS" your mom believes in teaches against it. I found that even he wants us to learn for ourselves. That's the only way to prove the truth of anything. Look it up in the dictionary or research it yourself. Whatever it takes, as long as the evidence dictates the answer." I didn't go any further for fear of hurting her feelings. I just hugged her and said that I needed to get back to my ending, which she was now in. She just grinned from ear to ear. I did finish by telling her that I wasn't picking on her or her family and how I love them dearly. I was only sharing knowledge of my "DISCOVERY."

"I believed in god for a lot of the same reasons you do, baby girl. And, I also scientifically believe in conquering death and going to heaven! But the god story is confusing and it doesn't make sense to me. That's why I'm writing this book.

I'm going to solve our mystery!" I said boldly as I hugged her one last time and got back to the book. I couldn't tell her I was just trying to point out religion's powerful effect on people world-wide. It not only happens with children, but with major countries all over the world, too. The USA is a Christian-dominated religious country. I didn't tell her what I really knew.

The scary thing is that the majority of the earth is ruled by leaders who believe in religion and their creation stories. And yet, they know the definition of the atom and energy. What's going on? This "CONTRADICTION" begs to be questioned. They are supposed to be leaders of a free world, where we all know knowledge should rule. This belief in "GOD" creating the universe is a provable contradiction! If you don't believe me, ask a god believer who created the atom and see what I mean. They just don't get it! What's wrong with them? I "Think." I know. Because most if not all live a contradiction I detest. These leaders are wealthy and yet glorify the working poor. Their mind is diseased by religion and wealth. They don't see the scientific contradiction to their faith and definitely don't see that religion is anti-wealth, either. Science works for the common good of all humans. Therefore as a scientist, I am giving all my money to the poor and challenge everyone to do the same. Don't think this isn't powerful; it is the ultimate test to pass!

Before you read any more, I must warn you that I "FOLLOW" only the evidence and it tortures me. You will know why, when you read the rest of my story. But it also gives me hope. I'll explain at the end of this letter. I can assure you that the content of this book is just as graphic, real, and harsh as the covers implies. I used the atom and the Jewish Star of David on the back not only because it is the final frontier of knowledge, but also in hopes that kids could see the scientific future ramifications of these two symbols matching. It epitomizes the urgent need for understanding where we came from and where we are going. We now live in a time where we can destroy ourselves, just as the Jewish story predicts! This can't be ignored when their symbol matches the very thing we can destroy ourselves with. NUCLEAR SCIENCE!

Although the front cover is not a subject matter for kids, our ancient ancestors left these ancient artworks to tell our human story. This picture is worth more than a thousand words and is a key piece of the puzzle in solving our mystery. It not only clearly shows the brutal and torturous human condition and why they stay away (we kill for sex), but also depicts the mixture between these heavenly beings and man I mentioned earlier. Notice the bald head like an alien and the body of man. Could this prove primitive man's god was an alien, addicted to the power of human uniqueness in looks and that they did, in fact, mix? I asked myself more science/future questions. Or are they so medically advanced that they have the ability to transplant memory from one human body to another, giving us reincarnation traditions and the power they so desperately crave? Have they achieved immortality of the mind scientifically? Did they mix their DNA with primitive man's, to give us the different races, as if competing to make the most beautiful species? I had so many questions. But inevitably, I couldn't deny my own addiction to outward beauty.

This may sound crazy, but there are ancient mother-goddess statues sharing this same evidence. Moreover, the yin and yang looks like two sperm in an egg, supporting this possibility. It's an indisputable fact that lust for sexual power is our society's number one addiction, and if heaven mirrors earth, then maybe it's theirs, too. The ancient religious writings universally say so. I even found that "JESUS said there was only one thing above humans, angels. They are all "EQUAL" and don't give their hand in marriage. The heads of Easter Island all look the same, like the rest of nature's creations. I couldn't find any that didn't look the same, from a school of bass to a flock of geese! We're the "ONLY ONES" who all look different. Could our mystery be all about who can be the prettiest and who has the most power? "PRETTY POWER," I call it. They usually go hand in hand; we all know that. Does Anna Nicole Smith ring a bell? I knew I was addicted to beauty and I had déjà vu. I found all "NORMAL" people were. We only seem to care less if were close to dying! Did the angels/gods/extraterrestrials evolve from the atom, which is the universal invisible god story, and create humans for outward power? This tantalizing question ate at me like a cancer.

Anyway, back to my story! The ancients'

religious stories and this ancient statue make it "crystal" clear how sexually addicted to power that these heavenly beings/extraterrestrials are. We know how addicted to it we are; just turn on the television or the internet. Sex sells everything! Lucky for us though, the ancients had no problem with nakedness. They used it in these artworks to tell their children the story of our origins. Unfortunately, however, we do! Not only have we sugar-coated them and stretched them beyond belief, but we have covered up the truth of them, as well. Even worse, we have covered ourselves up. Unlike them, we have made nakedness and sex even more perverted than ever. It's even our dirtiest word! How ironic that the dirtiest thing produces the most beautiful, huh? "EVERYONE" loves a newborn baby (if it's their own!). Come on, people, they live openly naked and many still do, without sex crimes. Only modern society is plagued with the horror of sexual crime against each other and even worse, our own children! I found that "civilization" breeds a terrible disease of sexual perversion and addiction!

This "ANCIENT CERNES GIANT" evidence and

life experiences answered Fermi's Paradox for me. It also helps explain why our mystery started and when their separation, which is my parents' god/devil story, began. I was taught that these heavenly beings are "PERFECT" and spirit. But are they? Why would spirits have sex, and what happened with their perfect story? For me, the facts are epitomized by the Cernes Giant on the front cover. The giant story is in every religion. They are a result of the angels/gods wanting and having sex with the "PRETTY" daughters of man. You know my take on it by now! Very soon, you will know the whole story and my short answer to the theory of everything. I am just about done. I am humbled by the amount of information I have learned and continue to learn.

Sadly, the power religion holds over my parents has kept them from reading the six books I've written. It will probably do the same with this one as well. Even though some of my family may have finished the first book, I doubt very seriously that any of them seriously think I could have solved the most sought-after prize in science, "The theory of everything," let alone the mystery of life. I was wrong, as I said earlier; I was finally having an impact on some of my brothers and their families. As for the rest, that's okay, I do understand why and certainly don't fault them for it. Heck, my mother is a treasure; how could I? I will cherish all of them forever, because I owe them everything, especially my mom! I understand that some people really just don't care about these answers. They're just trying hard to get through life the best way they know how, like my brother Brian. He cares, but just sees that it won't change things instantly or for everyone, anyway. Besides, life doesn't deal everybody as rosy of a hand as it did mine. I'M FORTUNATE AND GRATEFUL!

But if you do seek religious or scientific answers and don't give this a chance, then you may have already fallen prey to the "organization/ sheep" disease. I call it "The Jesus Paradox." You will see why as you continue reading. I've also found that it definitely applies to UFOlogy and science as well. The only cure for this disease is to follow the evidence and not the storyteller/organization. UFOlogy "FOLLOWERS" didn't believe me either, when I shared it with them at the international UFO conventions. I was dumbfounded to find the majority believing in a dimensional existence, just like spirit believers (third heaven). I haven't given up. I really feel this evidence solves Fermi's Paradox and proves the existence of these beings. I finally realized science was my only chance. Sadly though, my parents' religion said there is only one earth, and I'm afraid they might never consider life elsewhere possible! We are now finding potential earths almost on a daily basis, and it doesn't change them! Christianity now encompasses half the world's population and follows this dogma (brain-washing) technique.

Much to my horror, I also discovered that most aren't "SEEKERS" either, including myself. The evidence is clear: ONLY A MONK TRULY SEEKS AND, YES, HE/SHE CAN BE A SCIENTIST, TOO. I never became a monk (completely anyway; read my story). However, my parents really aren't any different from all the other religious followers, which is why I called my first book *The Two Witnesses and The Religion Cover-Up*. This is the Jesus Paradox. Everybody says they're looking for him, but no one would believe a person, or knows how to prove it if someone said they were. My story is a simple one and proves my point beautifully.

I was raised in a Christian household, so I started there. Besides, I don't think anyone in his right mind would argue against Jesus being the most famous person in human history. This I found to be the most obvious irrefutable fact of life. It made a huge impact on me as it has the entire world. I further found that all Christians are supposed to be looking for him, but no one believes I could be him. Even worse, my parents' religion "BELIEVES" that when Jesus returns his name will be Michael and when I went to them and asked if I could be him, they threw me out of their church! I would like to go back "UNDERCOVER" and film their violent reaction. A replay of this event, on film and in front of a jury, is the only possible cure to "WAKE" them. It is the only way to "SAVE" their children from the same violent behavior against someone else.

I do give my mom credit for at least entertaining this possibility, but she didn't know how to prove it, or not, either. I told her only the evidence can do that, Mom. I would simply be the messenger presenting it. She didn't really understand how to challenge me. I wish she would've watched, *The Day the Earth Stood Still*. The "SCIENTIST" knew how to challenge the alien: ask scientific questions! But with Mom, the evidence was the problem. I couldn't walk on water, turn it into wine, or raise the dead. That's what she was looking for. She didn't understand science. I so desperately wanted her to "SEE" and understand science. If she did then she could see that Jesus was giving us the "theory of everything" with his explanation of being born again (achieving immortality, being infinite).

I tried to explain this for her, but she didn't understand. I told her that he described it "like the wind, not knowing whence it comes from, nor where it is going."

"He further said," I continued slowly and methodically, wanting her to absorb the scientific significance of this parable, "that so will it be when he returns. This is a very clear example for infinity and omnipresence of the atom." I told her I used it with children and had done it with Madyson as well for this ending. It was perfect for children, and that is my goal. I want them to "KNOW

EVERYTHING—KNOW THE ATOM." They can understand water "COMING FROM NOTHING AND BEING NOTHING" but energy and information! Maybe they will understand the same thing about themselves?

Explaining "NOTHINGNESS" is the key, I told Mom delicately. This is a "DEEP" subject matter, and yet so "SIMPLE" at its core, that I think a child can understand perfectly. I explained to her that I told Madyson how I can take an ice cube and place it on hot pavement, watch it with her as it melts and disappears, but know she thinks it still exists. The reason is that when I asked her where it is, she, like all children, would always say "THE SKY." When I ask them if it stops existing, they would all quickly reply, "No, it's just the air now." I told Mom how this related to Jesus and the wind parable. A child's understanding of it was simply a direct result of science knowledge. They are taught to see the three states of matter and never question their infinite existence again. Unless religion takes over with its creation story. Science knows better. After all, we are made of water! What a beautiful thing!

"If only I could do this for you, Mom," I told

her as I hugged her. "It would be the greatest gift I could ever give you. Heck, Mom, what am I saying, I think I can." She hugged me back, really hard. I think she finally understood. Unfortunately, Mom also knows my final theory about the angels/aliens and is tortured by it as well. She has a hard time grasping life without the sexual nature of individual beauty. I am still trying to help her picture life from these heavenly beings' "EVOLUTIONARY/CREATION" perspective above, looking down on all the hell that our sexual nature brings us. She sees it, but her addiction to it makes it a torturous evidence to "WANT TO BELIEVE" just like the prophecy of the two witnesses! This amazing fact alone almost drove me insane. COULD I REALLY BE THE ONLY ONE TO SEE THIS? (Read my story to find out why only me and not the other witness!) If so, what if we have to make a choice when they "COME BACK" between being an alien in PARADISE/SPACE, where it's "BORING" or a human, where it's hell on earth. Be careful what you wish for, because it's obvious how "a-DICK-tive" human drama is. Look at the Cernes Giant and say sex, drugs and rock-n-roll! We all "KNOW IT" because we watch

"IT/POWER" every day on TV! Well, I imagine some don't.

Well, for those of you who don't know what the "theory of everything" is, like my mother and a whole lot of other people (including myself not too long ago), it is the holy grail of physical science and life itself. To finally answer what is surely impossible to most, seems unbelievable. But, not to me! I'm not being arrogant. It's just that my dad taught me, at a very young age, you could easily understand how something was made by taking it apart and putting it back together. We are doing this with human DNA! Now, I understand the Scripture of the first verse, in 1st John, "In the beginning was the word and the word was with god and is god." God is the atom and we are it! Now, I clearly see the religious confusion of Jesus being god vs. the son of god. He's both and everything, too. That would explain heaven being the universe. (Heaven is spread all around you and you just don't see it.)

Finally, "I LEARNED ABOUT THE ATOM" and solved our mystery. I often became angry at myself for discovering my ignorance of it and this theory for forty years. Heck, for that matter, even written history itself. It's now painfully obvious: Why it is so shockingly short! We are brutal against each other. Why didn't I see all this thirty years ago, when I learned it in science? I now know why and have let love conquer my shame. I forgive myself! I don't judge anybody else. I walked in their shoes and still do! I'm still learning. That's what is truly exciting.

I hope everyone can give me a chance because I am about to try and explain the "IMPOSSIBLE." I will attempt to explain how the evidence shows that these heavenly beings evolve infinitely and then live long enough to conquer immortality, scientifically. Conundrum? I don't think so. I am about to answer the age-old question, "DID WE HAVE A BEGINNING?" and explain how we do and, yet can be infinite as well! READ ON!

I can tell you that the answer will be in the form of a question, to my sons, at the very end. Amazingly and "THANKFULLY" I predict they will not only be able to answer it, but they will do it with their eyes wide open, in complete wonder, at the simplicity of it. Tears will be streaming down "MY" face, as they involuntarily rejoice in the joy of it. "FINALLY, NO LONGER WILL THEY WONDER

IF DEATH IS THE END." They will not only believe it is possible to overcome, but "BELIEVE" it has been, like science predicts and religion professes, to be so! My hope is that they will then ask me what it's like in heaven and listen. I will show them the space station and ask them to think infinitely beyond it. They will gaze upon it in awe of this "REALITY" and there will be only one "MIRACLE" left. They will choose "THE WAY" of heaven, scientifically!

I know I'm proposing to fill a tall order and wouldn't do so if the evidence didn't "COMPLETELY" answer all the questions about our mystery. Even though it does for me, check them for yourself. DON'T TAKE MY WORD FOR IT! FOLLOW THE EVIDENCE.

I lost my dad ten years ago and will soon lose my mother. My children will soon lose me and so on, and so on. My goal became and is to conquer death for everyone! Is it possible? Religion says so; science says so; I say so! This journey has taken its toll on my family and everyone around me. For this, I am so sorry and am crying as I write this. It has taken its toll on me, as well. My heart is heavy and filled with great regret. I have terrible memories of the pain and had no "RIGHT" to inflict the fear of death on my children. I don't want to be sad anymore. Seeking answers alone can become one's "organization" if you aren't careful. My story epitomizes this point beautifully. Please let me explain, with complete humility, deep regret and much sadness.

You see, I thought I was just innocently sharing the facts of my search along the way. But I wasn't. I not only was forcing it on them (more like shoving it down their throats), I was unknowingly paving my road to heaven with this hell and even inflicting it on everyone along the way. Especially myself, because I will have to watch my own film, like the Jehovah's Witnesses, and swallow some of my own medicine! I need to just let it go. I love children and want so badly to keep them from such a dreadful subject matter. Thankfully, throughout this whole ordeal, I don't think I have attacked anybody, but I did gave a new meaning to the old saying "the road to hell is paved with good intentions." I was now living my own hell, called regrets! Well, since hindsight is 20/20, I now must admit that I did shamefully and regretfully attack someone. The worst attack imaginable.

I attacked the most precious thing in my life, my sons. Old sayings, sadly, keep coming true in my case. I did hurt the ones I loved the most. "WHY?" My "GOOD" intentions won't ever take back the pain I caused my youngest son, as he expressed his fear of death to me. It doesn't matter that I was trying to show him evidence of a flying saucer, which proved to me life had conquered space already and does exist. I was even jubilant when I begged him to quit crying, because they've conquered death too. Ultimately, I was trying to tell him that this matching evidence proves they are the heavenly beings religion writes about. It didn't matter, because he cried out in fear of my anger and I didn't even hug him. I was so caught up in wanting to prove "MY POINT" that my anger toward his lack of respect for my evidence, caused me to lose my empathy for him. "HOW COULD I DO THAT?" Why did I have to constantly remind him of death? How could I have been so self-centered and blind to his feelings? I felt like shit then and I still do now! I couldn't even bring myself to share anything with him anymore. I was so ashamed and tortured! I started telling him every day that I love him and was sorry. I tried to hug him as much as I could. He didn't let me much, but I was thankful for every one I got! I "NOW" try to never say I'm sorry anymore, because it only reminds us of our pain again. I've learned to let it go. My sons are very forgiving, and I am forever grateful for that. I love both of my boys so much!

Even though I continue to film flying saucers and see them, I've proven to myself that there is no perfect world/universe. The universe is a harsh and chaotic place, where Mother Nature rules "NOW." Everybody knows that she can't be beaten. But can "SHE?" "HEAVEN" could only "SCIENTIFICALLY" exist in an artificial setting like a spacecraft or man-made planets. Remember Stephen Hawking's statement in the beginning. Again, I use the Stephen Hawking rule, because it exists now; it is happening in the "SPACE STATION." It must exist everywhere! Ironically, we see now how natural disasters can't take us out like man-made disasters can. We just saw Japan nearly get wiped out, by the world's fourth-largest earthquake in recorded history! But it pales in comparison to a nuclear catastrophe.

We are on the verge of a nuclear meltdown like Chernobyl. It brings home the Scripture's point on the back cover.

However, my continuous sightings of flying saucers gives me "INFINITE" hope life does exist infinitely and the possibility of conquering death is a reality. "WE EXIST NOW." This is the most important evidence to learn for curing any doubt that we will continue to do so. Now I am crying tears of joy! Thank you, Stephen Hawking, thank you, flying saucers, for matching the ancient cave drawings! Your spacecraft hasn't changed over tens of thousands of years! I was actually shouting "UP" in thin air.

This is "ROCK SOLID" evidence of their omniscience and omnipresence! The omnipotence factor I still had a problem with. The "EVIDENCE LEADS ME" to a simple conclusion as to why they "ALLOW" this "HELL" to exist! But that doesn't mean I have to like it. "FRANKLY" in my humble opinion, all fathers would make the world perfect, if they could. Again, just ask any father whose child is dying of cancer, if you don't believe me. I know I'm a father and I would! I not only would, but am clinging to the hope that I will see Nancy Gail, Danny, Dad, Granny, Dave, Terry and all my loved ones who have passed, again. Tragically enough, there are way too many to keep mentioning. This is the saddest reality of life, death itself. I will help to conquer death! The Bible itself and the Biblical story of Adam is really all about life after death. Hope springs eternal in my house, and this evidence proves this possibility. After all, Adam is made up of atoms. We are atoms/Adams and they are infinite. I will see them again!

Last, but certainly not least, please think about my theory "INFINITE ASTRONAUTS" infinitely! Where did they come from? If your answer is god, then where did god come from? I said earlier that I will answer our mystery by asking my sons a question. But before I do, I want to dedicate this to my parents for being there for me, no matter what. Even though my dad went overboard with his temper, I knew he would die for me if he could make the world perfect. I also want to thank my children, as well as all the children of the world, for giving us adults the only "PURE LOVE" we get. Furthermore, I beg forgiveness from everyone, but especially my two sons. I owe it to them, "REMEMBER." If you decide to read my whole story, please overlook my self-righteous, babbling redundant brainstorming. Really, I don't mind being wrong. (I just saw where I was wrong about gold, in one of my previous books!) I'm just hoping "COMMON SENSE" is the only "SENSE" you take away from this and not my two cents. Believe me, we all have it in "COMMON" "IF WE LET IT WIN." It's called the "SIXTH SENSE."

I will, now reconcile destiny vs. free will and answer our mystery. I sometimes often wonder if I am different, because I was the "SIXTH" child. Man was created on the sixth day, the giants have six fingers, the alien autopsy did too, etc., and mankind, also called mystery/whore, is numbered 666! The atom and the Jewish Star of David not only match, but have six points! There are many more weird coincidences like this in my books. You'll have to read them to find out!

In retrospect, I look forward to the day science rules. Please, let's all put aside our differences and give our children a chance to make the world a better place than what we leave it for them. They have enough to overcome as it is. Our greedy industrial past has ravaged the earth and unbelievably, we are still polluting it, at an unimaginable pace, even in the face of watching an impending ticking clock of self-imposed planetary death. Even worse, the nuclear struggle is tragically "UNFOLDING" before us. We have nuclear power plants on every continent that nature can "THROW" into a chain reaction of meltdowns and yet, we can't stop it. Our nuclear weapons won't touch this catastrophe. This we can stop, or "CAN WE?"

And throughout all this horror, I have become as obsessed with challenging religion's spirit teaching, as the famous magician Houdini. Unknowingly, he used Stephen Hawking's rule to discern that spirits didn't exist, because he never got to see his mother again. Therefore, since he didn't get to see the incredible scientific achievements we've made today, I am compelled and honored to carry his torch. Like me, he loved his mother dearly, too! He was also Adamant in stating that all magic was born of natural processes! For him, I want to answer what became of his mother. Like him, I detest the way religion preys on the religiously weak. I heard Pat Robertson, a TV preacher, asked by a viewer the other day on his television show *TBN*, "if god was a spirit or man?" He said god is a spirit, just like the "BIBLE SAYS." This is still "THE QUESTION" to be answered, and I think Houdini would get the last laugh, well, say at least. Death is certainly nothing to laugh at.

My answer for him is the same as it is for Fermi's Paradox. The evidence says they're real flesh-and-blood beings like us. People, first of all, we are on the verge of scientifically achieving all ancient religious traditions, from creating new life forms to invisibility, and even reading each other's minds! "GOD FORBID" or we wouldn't even ask why they stay way. But I have to say that of all the ancient traditions, I love the act of looking up to heaven most. It is still done today every time a religious athlete scores! THIS IS WHAT DRIVES MY ANSWER TO BARBARA WALTER'S QUESTION, "WHERE IS HEAVEN?" It's the sky/space.

A spirit god who is omnipotent begs us to question "HIS" making the earth and life on it in six days. Why not instantly to substantiate his omnipotence? We can't ignore the obvious scientific fact that the Biblical story of creation is indeed,

"EVOLUTIONARY." The Judeo-Christian god story forces us to answer questions and contradictions like these with logic and reason. Religion gives us many scientific details that we are only finding out with today's technology. However, we continue to let the fear of "TRADITIONAL" retaliation stop us from learning the truth about ourselves. Moreover, will we even accept the truth if it tortures us like my dream and prophecy implies? I am about to take that step into the unknown and ask myself and my children the inevitable.

Could these angels/gods/god be aliens that evolved and all look the same? Have they become addicted to the power of manipulating outward beauty? Is it possible that they have created our species for this reason? Are power addicts, in bodies they control the destiny of, for "SELF-LEARNING" sake? All religions tell us to "KNOW THYSELF" and state clearly, "THOUGH YOU ONCE KNEW." WE HAVE UNIVERSAL REINCARNATION STORIES AND DÉJÀ VU. I propose that my own addiction to beauty makes this possible to me. I can't speak for you. But the scientific evidence to support this futuristic possibility is abundant in our past. It is also clearly visible in our future, on television everywhere. If you think not, then know this. Plastic surgery is the fastest growing field on earth, everywhere!

I want to end with an overwhelming fact I discovered during my "LIFE CHANGING" journey. It will explain all the clues I gave you throughout this story, about the importance of the Jewish messiah's name. Could we have "FREE WILL" and yet, our destiny be scientifically possible after all? Well, the evidence says personal decisions are not destined, but mankind's history and direction certainly seemed to be shaped by it. "IF" destiny is something which happened before and is controlled by an infinite intelligence's "NEED" to propagate itself, then there is a reasonable explanation as to how this can happen. It's obvious to me there can only be one reason. I will answer that with the question to my sons at the end.

Before I do, however, consider that Jesus is the most famous man on earth, who says he will be back to "SAVE" us and "THE EARTH" from us. "HE IS COMING FROM THE SKY." Now, also consider, that English, "COINCIDENTLY," is our number one language on earth and in space. Well, what if he comes back as an alien and ask us to "BELIEVE" in his destiny, because we must leave with him, to escape/"CONQUER" Mother Nature's impending wrath? Will we do it? His story is one of destiny, as the Gospel Scripture clearly states: "THIS CHILD IS SET FOR THE RISE AND FALL OF ISRAEL." I have asked, apprehensively, myself, the question that I am about to pose to the world. I will also ask my children, after I explain how destiny and choice is possible.

"SONS," "IMAGINE" waking up in an "INFINITELY" futuristic setting. You're in a spacecraft or artificial planet and all this is a bad "DREAM." You suddenly realize you're an alien whose species has evolved from the ATOM/"NOTHING" and lived to be thousands of years old. Because you all look the same, have no religion, and "POSSESS" an infinite knowledge of your existence, you suddenly realize Mother Nature/space and death has been conquered! Wait a minute! You find out that you are immortal and yet you have a beginning. How is this possible?

Well, your species has become what we call

gods, to know they've always existed! They've proven, like we are now, that life evolves wherever the sun shines! But, then the worst happened; they began to desire power over one another. Power to control "themSELF" and have outward power through beauty of the flesh. They know there is only one way to have it, since they're all equal in looks and yet sexual. They artificially create mankind and become us, to experience our intoxicating power over one another. They forbid our creation and quarantine us on earth, where we can serve a scientific purpose of harvesting precious metals and gems for life in space. Ultimately, the realization that our species would never exist without scientific creation causes them to intervene and stop our "DESTINED" self-destruction from happening. And when they do, we must do one thing upon their return. Cooperate and "BELIEVE" the truth about ourselves. This is how we are destined and yet have free will.

"WE AREN'T DREAMING." IT IS TIME TO "WAKE UP." We must accept heaven as space, because the earth is going to experience a terrible global catastrophe. Well, sons, sadly and wonderfully, this is the picture the evidence paints for me. Sadly, only because we are ignorant of the "UNIVERSE/HEAVEN" and life in it; wonderfully, because it has been conquered. Mother Nature, pain and death have all been scientifically conquered! "SPACE/HEAVEN" is their final frontier. They can't live with us, because they are real and still experience all three. It's just that in their "WORLD" they don't, because they are of "ONE" mind.

Now, if you can imagine living to be 14.5 billion years old, which the known universe is "DATED," let alone a thousand as the Bible says, then can you imagine how you would "LEARN" that your species always existed and your memory could too, through scientific creation? Wouldn't you know that you had a beginning in "FORM" that will live, die and always repeat this cycle of life, but you could "OVERCOME" death, to create "YOUR OWN" immortality?

They both looked at me and then looked at each other. Their eyes grew wide with excitement. I couldn't stop myself. I grabbed them both up and gave them the biggest hug I could. This time my youngest didn't resist. He hugged me back and said "Wow, Dad, I can easily see how that's possible, huh."

"It's not only possible, son. It's happening as we speak." I immediately reached and got a picture of the space station. "This is heaven," I said with tears streaming down my face. My oldest reached and hugged me.

"Don't cry, Dad, you'll see Terry again." He knew my pain because he knew Terry's love. My youngest was smiling as we both turned and hugged him, too. I felt his tears as my face pressed against his and I whispered in his ear.

"Don't cry, son; I know you love us and I know that you aren't scared of death anymore, either. Me and Terry both know." He knew that Terry believed more than anybody that I could have the answer to "THE THEORY OF EVERYTHING." I felt him hug both of us, like I hadn't felt in fifteen years. I was so happy. I think they believed me, too! As we broke apart, I told them I wasn't a bible thumper and they know that.

"But a world full of 'YESHUAS' is a pretty good place to be and he said it exists now, just like

Stephen Hawking. I'll leave you with one last quote to prove it.

"NO MAN WILL GO TO HEAVEN THAT DIDN'T COME FROM HEAVEN, EVEN THE SON OF MAN WHO IS IN HEAVEN, NOW."

"The universe is heaven. He was and is a quantum physicist telling us that we need to know the atom. We need to know $E=MC^2$! ENERGY equals/transforms into MATTER! The letters M stand for mass and C^2 for speed of light squared. When two atoms combine, they lose mass. This missing mass is released in the form of energy." They were a little puzzled, so I pulled it up on the computer.

"This is the Big Bang," I told them confidently. "The reason I think I have the answer everyone is looking for is because we're looking for the beginning of everything. It's kinda like the "STORY" I just told you to imagine about our "beginnings." How can we have a beginning if we know we always existed?

Well, the same thing applies to energy that came from this "TINY" singularity point of pure energy. Where did it come from and what is around it that we call 'NOTHING'? And what really kills me is that we know the atom and energy can't be created nor destroyed, right?"

"Yeah," they said in complete amazement as they just went back to their videogame. They both just looked awestruck. Hey, before you get lost in *World of Warcraft* I want to ask you again, before I go to work, the one question I'm asking of the world. And "REMEMBER" I'm doing this so we never forget and fear death, to help them understand the most important thing about life. It's "INFINITE."

"Come on, Dad," they grumbled, "give it a break, we 'BELIEVE' you. Okay?"

"Okay, but please repeat the question and prove you know your possible "INFINITE ASTRONAUT" existence, okay?

"If we evolved and lived long to make ourselves scientifically immortal, would we have a beginning?" they asked somewhat together. I was so "PROUD" of them.

"Great job remembering, guys. I'm so happy for you. Now, just don't forget it and pass it on to my grand-kids, would you!" I remarked loudly as I tackled both of them. We rolled around for a minute and got back up laughing. It was a beautiful moment. "Won't it be great to tell your kids they don't have to worry about death being the end?" I reaffirmed one more time as I struggled to get up. This time they didn't seem to mind as they went back to their videogame. I walked away with tears in my eyes. I love my family so much!

I'm now asking this question and more of the world. Think beyond the first question and our achieving immortality of our own species. The question of creation vs. evolution doesn't exist in our world. We know we evolved and our species is immortal, even if we wouldn't have conquered death, because of what we are made of. Atoms/Adams always exist again and again. In fact, think infinitely about curing the aging process, cloning ourselves, creating extra body parts, to new creation altogether and this question I'm about to ask now will make perfect sense to you, as it does to me. What if we know the only way to achieve individual immortality is through the idea of transplanting memory? Could this be what religion is all about? Isn't this the only thing that could torture us? We know "WE/THEY" won't always exist in the body of mankind, unless we achieve it scientifically. We can only "SAVE" our minds and have to let go of our individual egos as mankind. Mankind is not a product of nature, just science. It is what my first real fictional book will be called, *Reality*! When this book takes off and you want to know what it's like in heaven, I will tell you about how they transplant memory into different bodies. How they live without marriage, knowing we are all of the same family/species. Most of all, how they read each other's minds. Again, "GOD FORBID," but I will tell you "EVERYTHING"!

I am now asking this "FUTURISTIC" question of the world. Could we be them: aliens/angels/gods, addicted to the beauty and power of their creation? That question, when asked of me, "Am I?" has only one answer: "I am." "REMEMBER" that I said one word will solve our mystery and it would finally reveal why the Jewish Messiah's name is important? Well, just apply his name to the last question I just asked of the world and you get your answer, "YES-HU-A."(His name has been fraudulently changed in history and this is his real name in every language. English is the world's language in space!) It definitely supports the universal evidence of us all being addicted to beauty. I think none of us would want to be uglier than what we are. We're all beauty addicts, in my opinion. I know I am, and I know all adults are. Kids are brutally honest about this as well. Don't kid yourself, everybody; it just a matter of "TIME" before the world "UNLOCKS" the voices in all our heads!

I can see this "A-DICK-TION" as the only logical answer to "BENEVOLENT BEINGS NOT INTERVENING." It can only be a result of our "IMMORTAL POWER HYPOTHESIS": SCIENCE CAN'T BE STOPPED! They obviously rehabilitate their lost/addicted species by quarantining us on planets/hells until we finally get it. "IT" is scientific knowledge, the only thing worth saving!

The religious evidence says we may be them addicted to the sexual power of human uniqueness in looks. I have put the "OWL MAN" as the first illustration of ancient alien artworks to bring home this point. Again, a picture truly is worth a thousand words. I'm sorry if you think you will have trouble explaining this to your daughter. I understand, because I have nieces. But, you need to seek help and do so. Mankind is sexually dangerous. It's time to start being "TRUTHFUL" to our children about ourselves.

At the end of the day, family is all we have. I hope you enjoyed this "THEORY OF EVERYTHING"/LETTER. I am presenting it to science and my children. To better understand where it all came from, check out the rest of my books. And please remember, I'm giving all my royalty proceeds, over what I said in the beginning, to everybody who buys a book or has bought any artworks from me. Money is the root of all evil, and we can use it to cure it. We have to make rich people "DISEASED." "DON'T STORE YOUR TREASURES UP ON EARTH!" So buy them, please. If you don't like it, I'll give you your money back.

Today, finally, we "SHOULD" no longer have a religious child or a scientific child ask where everything came from and their parents reply with an answer that they cannot explain. They will want to know where god and the atom came from. WE MUST SCIENTIFICALLY AND HISTORICALLY TELL THEM WHAT THEY ARE. God and the atom/Adam are one and they are infinite. All matter is made of atoms. Adam is made of atoms. *I am you, you are me and we are the eggman, we are the walrus, kookookachu kookookachu!* The gods/aliens are nature's creation/evolution and all look the same. Mankind is a scientific creation for outward power through beauty of the flesh and would never exist. We are the only species to look individually different.

It's time to stop the "OMNIPOTENT MAGIC SPIRIT" god insanity and think science future. Logically, if you can "IMAGINE INFINITY," then you can imagine, that we are "GODS!" It's obvious and provable that this is the way the universe works. We've obviously done this before. History/nature is repeating itself. The Cernes Giant story reveals the answer to why we are separated.

Here is my simple answer to the "THEORY OF EVERYTHING": IT'S ALWAYS EXISTED! Here is my simple answer to FERMI'S PARADOX, Immortal power Hypothesis (mankind is a scientifically unstoppable evil)! Here is my simple theory of what the universe is: an infinite expanse of matter that has created intelligence, through evolution, which conquered its own mortality and propagates itself throughout space. These are the gods of primitive man and they all look the same, like all nature. (See heads of Easter Island.) Their desire for power over one another led to the scientific creation of mankind and the separation of "HEAVEN"/space and earth.

Now I understand Shakespeare's saying the world is our stage and we are but its actors. The aliens/gods are real; mankind is their actor. My mind is god; "Heaven is our throne and the earth a footstool." In the words of John Lennon, "IMAGINE" that the saying by Yeshua is true; "HEAVEN IS WITHIN YOU...your mind/voice!" And thanks to whoever said this: "The mind is a terrible thing to waste." The gods don't waste minds; they recycle them like everything else in the universe. Knowledge is power, but wisdom is "LOVE"!

I also want to thank Michio Kaku for his explanation of a type-three civilization. For me, it is a beautiful example of scientifically rewriting religion's story. But, I don't understand him not seeing it as such. I just hope he can expand his thinking, for allowing the ancient and modern matching evidence to establish UFOs as extraterrestrial.

THIS MIGHT JUST START A LOGICAL DIALOGUE AMONG OUR RELIGIOUS LEADERS, SOME OF WHOM ARE LAWYERS, OBAMA! If we could only be so lucky, huh? Anyway, his opinion that we need the DNA as final proof of something existing is contrary to science. One word: "GRAVITY." If he could validate that these craft must be of extraterrestrial origin, it would stop scientists from continuing to mock UFOlogy as quackery. I don't know if he knows this, but he could easily support this hypothesis by establishing one well-known and indisputable fact among scientists as well as all the leaders of the entire earth. Air superiority makes them extraterrestrial.

We are a world at war and full of bad people who want to not only conquer us, but wipe us out. They don't because of our air superiority. It is what makes us the leader of the world. Whoever made these craft would rule "OPENLY," but they don't! They're benevolent, just like we are, to lesser nations. We don't wipe them out. Furthermore, I find it ridiculous for the world to not accept these UFOs as the very life that 55% of the world thinks exist. Moreover, why doesn't Michio and all the world of intellect see that the UFO story is what created our religious stories? The gods have a type-three civilization.

In conclusion, I can only rationalize that their inability to think infinitely and an obvious lack of scientific knowledge are the very obstacles they must overcome. We should be looking for space-craft much more advanced than ours, and that's what we are seeing. Most importantly, it's exact-ly what our ancestors saw. "PEOPLE," for "GOD'S" sake, I can still find and film you a UFO.

I now present my Infinite Astronaut theory to the world. Please learn about the atom, Adam! It is you and you are the universe! Thanks so much for giving "ME" a chance. I'm shocked that the world is still entrenched, in such a primitive, supersti-tious, Santa Claus-like religious setting. If you don't think it is, then just apply the same logic to your-selves, as parents, as you do to your god. Is it log-ical to pick favorites or just save one child out of a group in the midst of tragedy? Or even bigger than that, in fact the biggest of all, wouldn't you make the world perfect if you could? The sad real-ity is that religious people don't confront this logic, and if you try to get them to, it will create anger. Don't try; just make a theory to science and "LET IT BE." "IMAGINE THE WORLD WITH ONLY ONE RELIGION AND IT WAS SCIENCE." Oh, what a wonderful world it would be.

I'm not good with jokes, especially ones played on me. So, here's a joke that was played on me and I finally got over it. I moved South (LOL. I know I was a religious redneck! Special thanks to Jeff Foxworthy)! It's called my religious redneck joke. (Remember it could also apply to science and UFOlogy.) If you think you're right and all the other religions are wrong, then you might just be a religious redneck. But, if you're religious and don't see that you could be just like them, a religious redneck, then you are a religious redneck! LOL. The biggest joke is "ISRAEL BELIEVING" they are the chosen people and their little piece of land in this infinite universe is holy. Come on, people, this is a scary joke. This is why I labeled my book as the most dangerous ever. We are on the verge of Israel nuking Iran and a religious nuclear holocaust!

Oh yeah, what the government doesn't want you to know, is that, they are religious rednecks

(RELIGIOUSLY DISEASED) and know these aliens exist, but don't "SCIENTIFICALLY" have an answer, as to why, they don't openly contact or help us! Pretty bad, huh? Well it gets worst; most of them are preparing to "DEFEND" ourselves against them "WITH THE HELP OF THEIR GOD." This is the biggest joke of all. Remember, people, "AIR SUPERIORITY RULES".

In the words of Socrates, "ONLY WILL WE KNOW PEACE WHEN WE REPLACE KINGS WITH SCIENTISTS/PHILOSOPHERS." Please, leaders of the world, recognize the harm of religion's god story and wake up to challenge the "LOGIC" of it. Please learn about the atom/Adam. "NOW, PLEASE JUST IMAGINE THEY ARE EVERYBODY, YET ONE AT THE SAME TIME AND KNOWS WHERE HEAVEN IS...SPACE/UP!"

Peace, Love, and harmony.

"FORGIVENESS ALWAYS!"

"MICHAEL"

P.S. Besides my parents, family and friends, this final book is also dedicated to the re-opening of the Tyler abduction case in the movie "THE FOURTH

KIND." Put yourself in her shoes! How would you like to have your baby taken from you? I always refer people to a good movie that best sums up our nature or situation. Since, this is the end of the road and my next book is called *Reality*, I recommend the reality show survivor. You can't win being honest. Go figure, huh! It's all about the money, too!

"LOVE ALWAYS"
to Portia Michaels Perez,
my god-daughter

Notice alien-looking head and obvious connection to sexual power addiction of man's body.

Infinite Astronauts?

Could our sudden appearance without the skull evolution from an elongated cranium to the obvious upright bulbous large head be directly related to religion's god? Our short recorded history is!

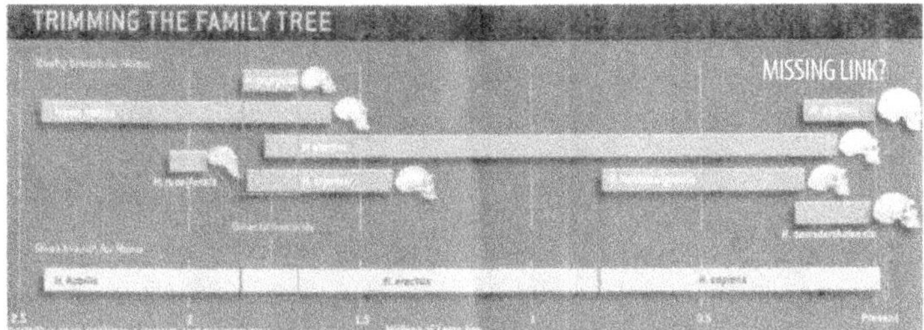

Could the large-headed statues below be primitive man's god/angel, and nature's creation/evolution? Nature does create life through evolution that looks "equal," like a flock of geese, a herd of zebras, etc.

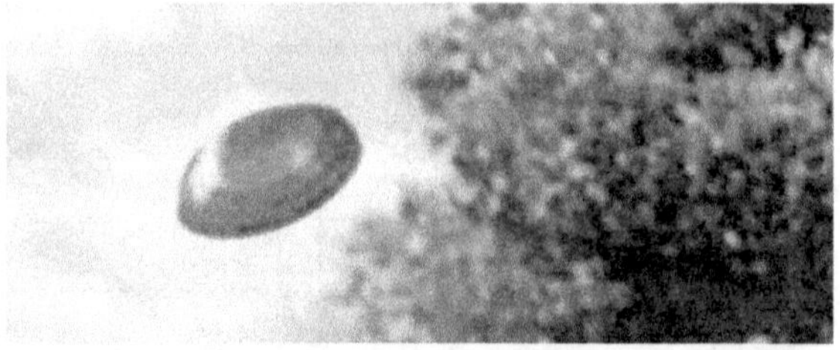

Paul Villa photo of flying saucer circa 1960.

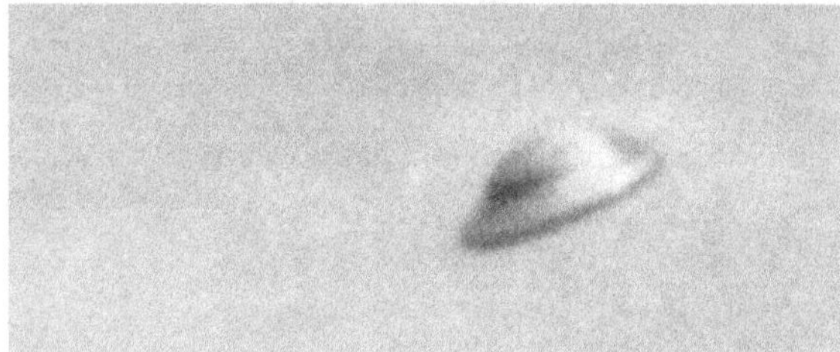

Picture on front cover of third and fourth book. How can these match when they are taken twenty years apart. Again, these "MATCH" ancient cave drawing on front cover. World's largest saucer on head of Easter Island, and aborigine saucer and alien's gold halo above (back cover) protecting it in space.

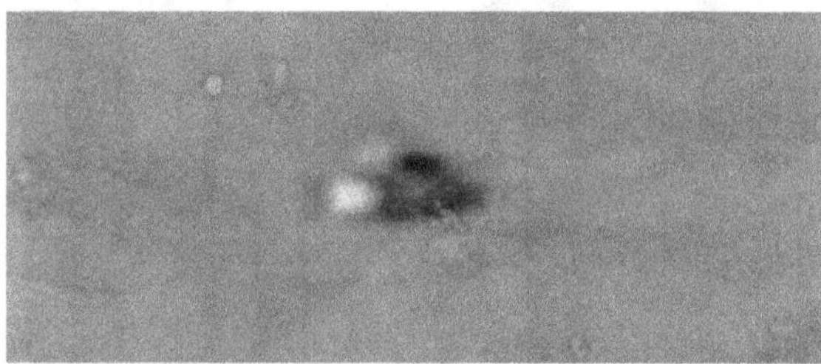

Video taken in 2003 by Jeff Willes of Phoenix, Arizona. To buy video, type his name in computer or call 623/847-9132.

Video taken in 2006 by Mike Brumfield in Phoenix, Arizona.

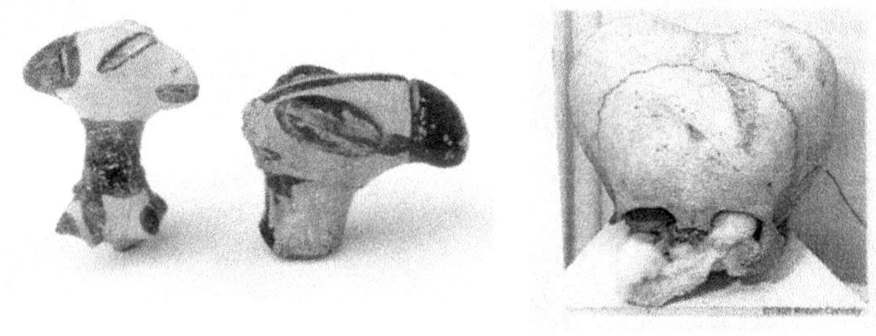

Oldest rock art on record catalogued by the Leakeys, ca. 50,000 years old, from Africa. Clearly shows little alien highlighted in box. It also shows another taller species restraining one of their own. The two heads above it were found in modern-day Israel, and are Sumerian; approximately 10,000 years old. The skull (from Peru) also supports ancient rock art of aliens in Africa. There are universal religious stories of two creations of man. Does this give us proof that they first tried to manipulate their own species to serve their needs?

Oldest Sumerian/Ubaid "God" statues on record in Museum of Antiquity, Cairo, Egypt. Clearly shows male and female gender and alien-looking beings. Picture, lower left, even shows mother nursing baby. Zechariah Sitchin claims these are android robots. They are, for God's sake, real "PARENTS!" If these are the most ancient statues that don't look like us, could they be primitive man's universal god/angel? Look at "Mother Goddess" statues on the following pages. They clearly are the god/angel that mixed with the "pretty daughter" of man.

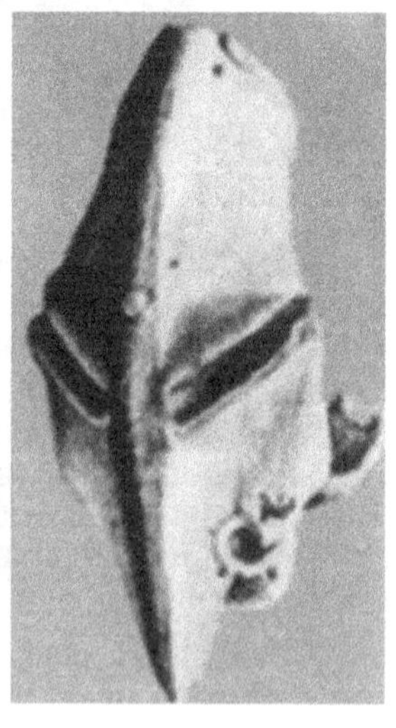

Ancient Sumerian King and Queen and Priest. Notice Priest has bald head—indicative of Alien God. Also notice big eyes.

The Sumerians carved statues of the gods from stone. From the statues we can see what they thought the gods looked like. Many gods looked like short people with round bellies. They had thin lips and big noses. They wore skirts made of sheep's wool. In fact, many statues of the gods looked like the statues the Sumerians made of themselves!

What Did the Sumerians Believe About the Meaning of Their Lives?

The gods of Sumer looked like men—and they acted like men. The gods liked good food and nice clothing. They got married and had children. Sometimes they were kind. Sometimes they were cruel. Either way, the Sumerians believed they had no control over what the gods did. Rather, the Sumerians believed that they were slaves of the gods. This story tells why.

THE SUMERIAN STORY OF THE CREATION OF MAN

The gods had always worked for a living. But when the goddesses were created, the gods had to work even harder to keep them happy. Then the gods had great trouble getting enough bread to eat

This is the oldest known historical record of Mankind's "God" story. It clearly shows they were real flesh and blood people. It also shows they created Mankind to work for them. This is an excerpt from an educational text called *Ancient Civilizations*.

Mother goddess statue from Catayal (modern-day Turkey), ca. 8000 B.C. It clearly shows an alien head representing God and a beautiful woman. This story is also universal in religion and reflects Gods/angels mixing with "pretty" daughters of man.[o]

These were found in Iraq. They are ancient statues of gods. Proves they have children, just like statues of alien parents holding child.

Cloning! Two squiggly lines, DNA!

These look like head of mother goddess statue and again connects aliens to Pyramids like evidence from Erich Von Daniken's book, *Gold of the Gods*.

More examples of "God" statues emphasizing "Big Head" and eyes. See how indentation in the forehead matches Iraq's statues. The top one (from Iraq) even has six fingers like other succeeding "God" statues. The bottom one is from South America.

These gold artifacts are from Erich Von Daniken's book *Gold of the Gods*.

Gold artifact from ancient mine in Peru. Notice two alien-looking beings holding snakes and third one at top inside pyramid. The circles look like flying saucer stem cells, atoms or eggs that are fertilized.

This connects pyramids to aliens. The pyramid served as image of rock that contained gold, quartz.

Alien-looking figure, right, has pyramid on head, penis and snake/DNA halo. The Bible says (Luke 6:4) "Only the Father in Heaven is God." Are these the fathers of heaven? Erich theorizes the skeleton on left could be a coded disk for message to contact future man. It is made of aluminum and coated in gold. We sent a coded disk into space with the same composition. I, again, see DNA, cells/eggs and chromosomes. The skeleton's head has a halo around it. See horned face like Africa rock art and Israel statures. The skeleton represents our deadly creation.

This is the most important evidence because it shows us, what their gods looked like (aliens), what they came and live in (flying saucers) and why they needed gold (space life and exploration). Hence we have the Biblical quote "Heaven's streets are paved with gold." It is a universal religious theme. Heaven is space, up to primitive man.

Cave drawing of aboriginal god Wandjina. Notice similarity to Owl Man. Also see halo around above head. This supports 10th planet story of gold replacing ozone and "who" was mining it before they created man as a "tiller of the ground" in Genesis. Man's purpose supports skeletal discoveries in gold mines. Gold protects astronauts from dangerous life radiation in space.

MOST IMPORTANTLY This solves pyramid mystery. Gold is found most in quartz which forms natural pyramid shape.

Religious statues by Olmecs from Mexico. They are also known for mysterious carvings of huge heads!

Figure circled is made of red lava rock like Easter Island man doing mystery. This is what power struggle of gods is about, us. Red symbolizes creation. Notice opposing sides black and white like Easter Island Man and Yin and Yang. Notice six obelisks like stones. Coincidence? Don't think so. Notice similarities to Easter Island statues, Israel statues, aborigines, all other "big headed" God statues from every continent.

The figures are all black and white "facing" each other. The one in the back that is porous looking is the only red one. Could this represent the power struggle over mankind's inevitable creation and does it involve the sixth chromosome? Also, notice the clear resemblance to the alien statue from Israel and the head on the mother goddess statue as well. It clearly looks like the Easter Island heads except for the elongation. They are the product of the mix between the sons of gods/aliens and man. I think losing the bulbous head was the first indicator of their pursuit toward outward beauty. The story supports this with their reason for mixing in the first place. (See back cover)

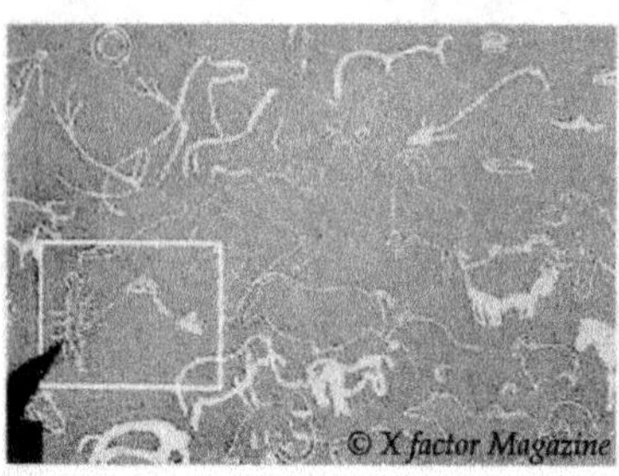
© X factor Magazine

Japanese discovery on the island now known as Taiwan. It is a drawing by a general that discovered a strange ship on the island. This happened in 1806! Notice the ships drawn above it. He found this drawing on the hull of the ship. The writing looks like the hieroglyphics found on the aboriginal gods halo and supports the description of Roswell's.

The cave art clearly shows matching saucers. This is dated circa 15000 years old. It is in France. It shows smaller ships coming out of a large one and abduction! The lines represent the invisible energy taking the human up. The top right picture is the oldest rock of aliens from Africa date circa 50000 years old. It shows the little alien/Roswell gray in control observing. He's even protected by a box that looks much like a tree trimmer's carriage. The others are larger and restraining one of their own. They must have first made themselves larger to be more able to control their scientific manipulations of primitive man. They are obviously serving the little guy and they are struggling with one of their own. Anyway, this supports the scientific manipulation of themselves. See the one with the horns. Is this what gave us the first images of the biblical "devil". Read on! See similarity to statues on following page.

These reptilian looking skulls are found in Ubaid, Iraq. They look like the reptilian looking tall ones on the rock art of the previous page. Scientists have repeatedly mistaken the eyes for sunglasses or goggles. However they are very similar to the large slanted eyes of the Roswell gray alien. They are identical to the eyes of the mother goddess statue from Israel. Notice one is a divided looking skull, giving it the appearance of hornlike appendages, while the other is elongated. They are clearly two different types. Were these a product of the first attempts to make themselves larger for power or for mining gold. Anyway, it is clear here and in the writings that scientific creation was producing things like this, the mothman, centaur and other abnormalities. The little guy with a HUGE head is from Utah! See appendages (Devil's horns?).

The Starchild controversy

SINCE FEBRUARY 1999 a bizarre looking skull, known as the Starchild skull, has been exhibited at UFO conferences and heavily discussed in UFO journals.

The Starchild skull is alleged to be the remains of an alien-human hybrid.

Legend of the Star People

According to the Starchild Project, an organization that wants to arrange DNA testing of the skull to prove an incredible origin, the skull was discovered in the mountains of northern Mexico. Indian tribes from the region have legends of Star People – beings from the sky who visit Earth to impregnate local women before returning years later to retrieve the hybrid infants.

Big head

The skull has several strange features that suggest it is not human. It has a massive brain capacity, flattened rear, shallow eye sockets, and is missing the front sinuses.

The Starchild Project claims to have consulted over 50 experts, the vast majority of whom argue that the skull is that of a deformed human child.

Most experts say that the Starchild skull is that of a child suffering from hydrocephaly, a disease in which fluid builds up on the brain and makes the skull swell.

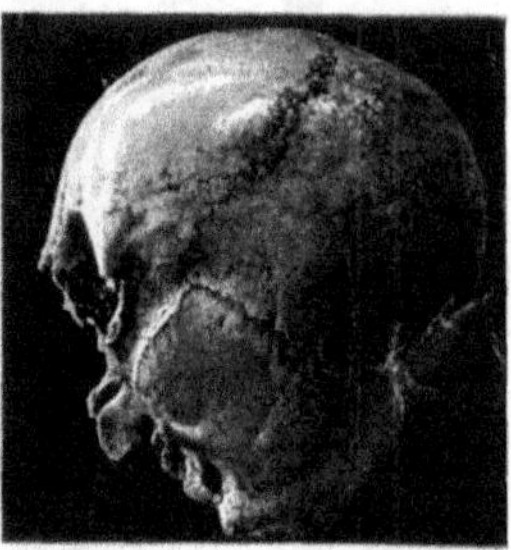

■ The Starchild skull *is far from normal. But is it from an abnormal or cradle-boarded human infant, or perhaps an alien–human hybrid?*

It is also widely thought that the skull has been cradle-boarded. Cradle-boarding is the practice of strapping an infant's head to a board and causes flattening of the back of the skull. It was practiced in the area of Mexico where the skull comes from. The Starchild Project argues that close examination of the skull rules out this explanation, and is attempting to raise funds to pay for DNA testing – the only way to be certain of the skull's origins.

"Beings from the sky" Is this the Owl Man which looks like an alien? He is pointing up! The skull supports this reality. Also "impregnates women" supports the cover art of the mother goddess statue, yet also has a big head! Skull is evidence of aliens being flesh and blood and these "sons of God" in Genesis 6:4. It supports my theory that they are not religious "spirit" magical beings. However, I conclude the atom, which makes everything, is "religion's invisible spirit" creator, evolving scientifically through time, not by magic. Read on. It scientifically fits religion's invisible omnipresent God.

Giants of Easter Island South Pacific

Notice the saucer on top of head tells us where they live just like owl man, aboriginal god, and Starchild legend spaceships just like on covers! They live up in saucers! Six strands of rock looks like DNA readouts. It also could implicate the sixth chromosome mystery or the Jewish creation on the sixth day. Giants were the offspring of gods and "pretty" daughters of man. This is when our separation occurred because wickedness spread all over the earth. A great flood followed. This is a red figure that symbolized mankind. See how he is doing the mystery or transcendental meditation, and looking up!

The six strands of rock below the Alien looking god could symbolize a DNA readout. I am intrigued by it being six strands. The day of man's biblical creation is the 6th. The Hopi prophecy has six beings (five of man, one of an alien). The hummingbird of the owl man in Nazca reflects this theme as does the biblical "devil". Is it possible that the sixth chromosome is the source of this "looks' manipulation. I've been reading a fascinating book called "The Sixth Chromosome". There are many other things pointing to creation involving the number six like the atom and Jewish star's number of points. The planet mars is the sixth from the tenth. There's more read on! Also, look at man meditating/doing mystery. He is made of red lava rock and is similar to many other representations of first religious worship. Red also represents blood and creation. Mystery worship is universal from Buddhism to sitting Indian style. Also notice black moai that looks somewhat different from the whiter standing ones. This parallels black and white yin and yang. It also parallels Olmec statues.

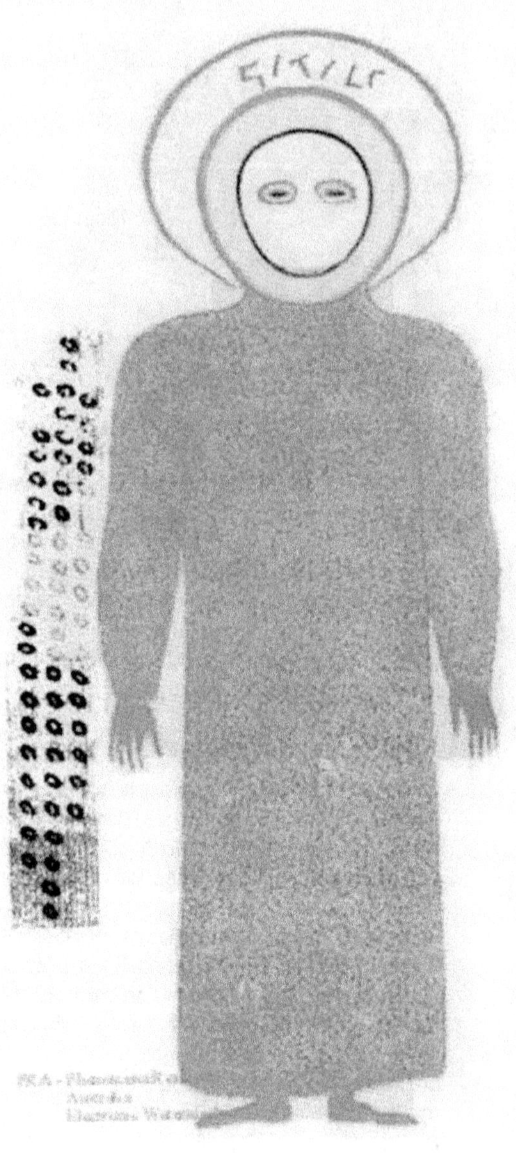

Aborigine cave drawing dated circa 30000 years old. Notice hieroglyphics on gold halo. Also notice readout similar to Easter Island one .These rock layouts/DNA readouts are common across the earth. Looks like scientist/astronaut in robe!

The bronze statue is from Kiev and is circa 8000 years old. It has six fingers supporting the existence and authenticity of the Roswell Alien autopsy. The recovered dead alien had six fingers and toes. This figure also supports the need for gold as protection in space. It has a Halo. Compare it to the following aboriginal gods. They look alien and even have gold painted halos around their heads. The Aztec block shows two hands intertwined with six fingers. These hands alone represent their god's creation of them and the entanglement represents DNA, how they were created. These match our medical symbol, intertwined serpents. How can they match when it takes an electron microscope to see them? The gods must be scientifically advanced!

Australian rock art compared to same in Utah.

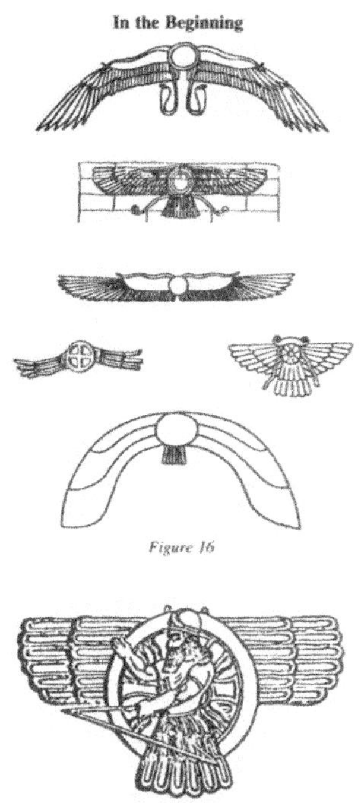

Figure 16

Figure 17

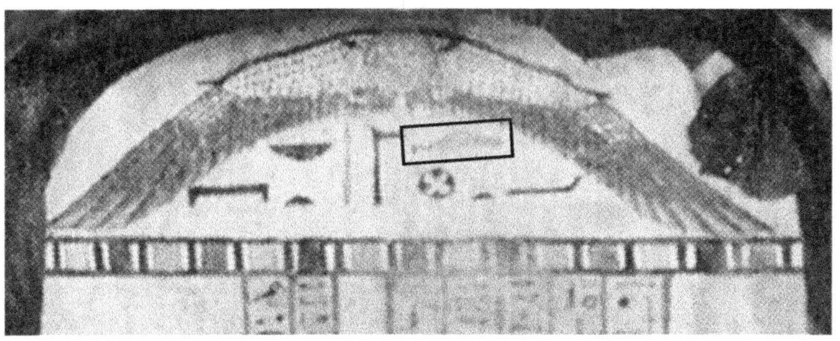

Ancient God symbolizes a flying saucer! These are all ancient symbols for god from Sumeria, Babylonia, Assyria, to the Egyptian one at the bottom. It has an actual saucer below the omni-present symbol of god which could literally be called a flying saucer. They all share this characteristic! Now we know why they're everywhere. But remember the atom is also a circle that is "every-thing". The Egyptian god is Atum! Notice the snakes for DNA creation. Also notice the cross symbol. It is the oldest geometry on earth representing the 10th planet. The Assyrian one clearly shows how man put himself in the circle. He became god!

Famous NASA Tether Incident

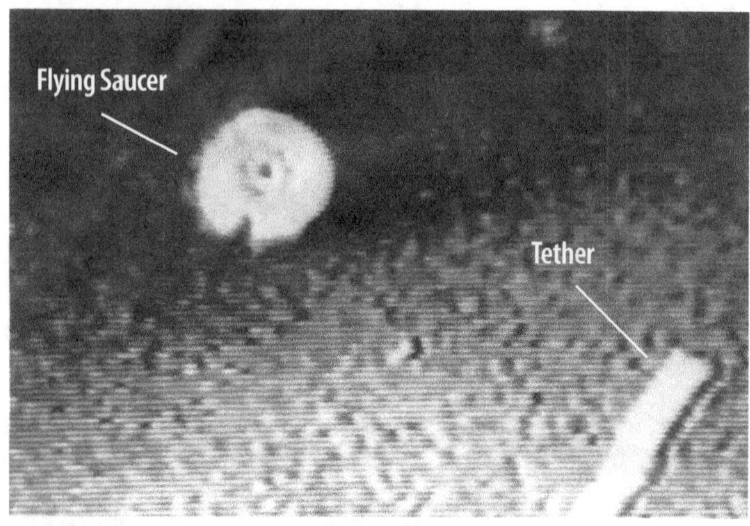

Saucer looks like galaxy, yin and yang, and the atom.

Galaxy has black hole in center which emits white matter.
See yinyang similarity.

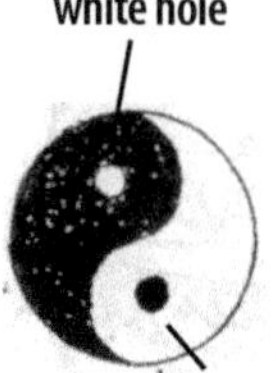

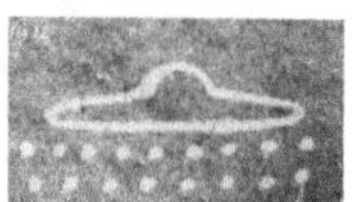

Cave drawing showing
saucer moving up

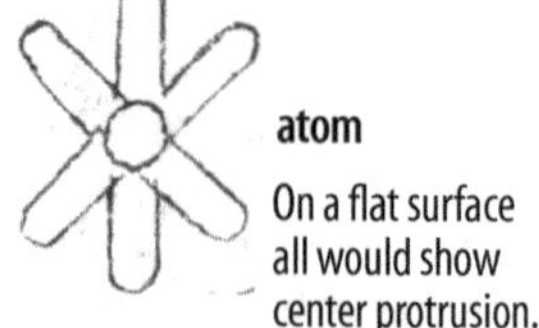

atom

On a flat surface
all would show
center protrusion.

Could spinning be key to anti-gravity? Is Event Horizon proof time can be stopped? Can all life be related to atomic structure? Does knowledge of atom answer life's mystery?

Famous NASA Tether Incident

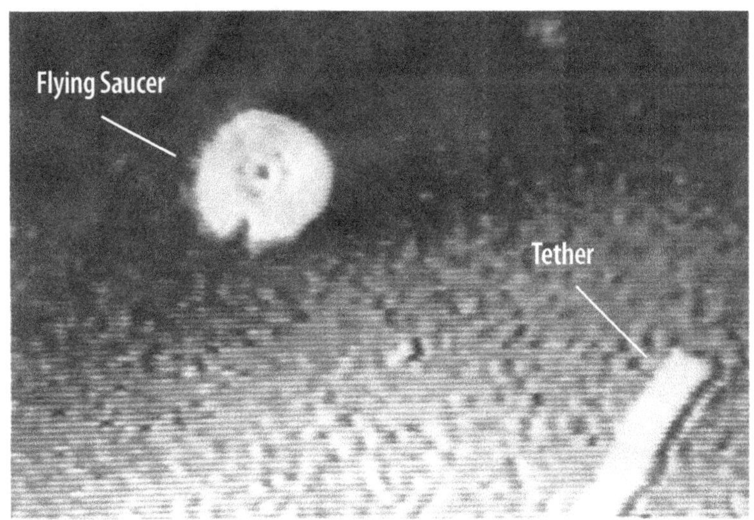

"Ancient" bronze disk from Norway. Gold overlay of sun, moon and objects in sky. The holes on outer perimeter look just like ones on disk from Turkey, Ohio and notches from Dropa stones. Notice seven circles like atoms between sun and moon!

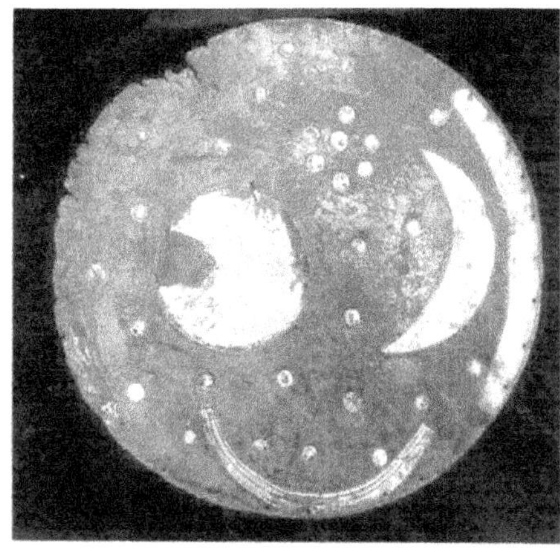

Notice the similarity of disk sculpture with indentation to flying saucer photograph by NASA. Most importantly, sculpture is in gold, which is what we use in the construction of our spacecraft today.

"Ancient" bronze disk from Norway. Gold overlay of sun, moon and objects in sky. The holes on outer perimeter look just like ones on disk from Turkey, Ohio and notches from Dropa stones. Notice seven circles like atoms between sun and moon!

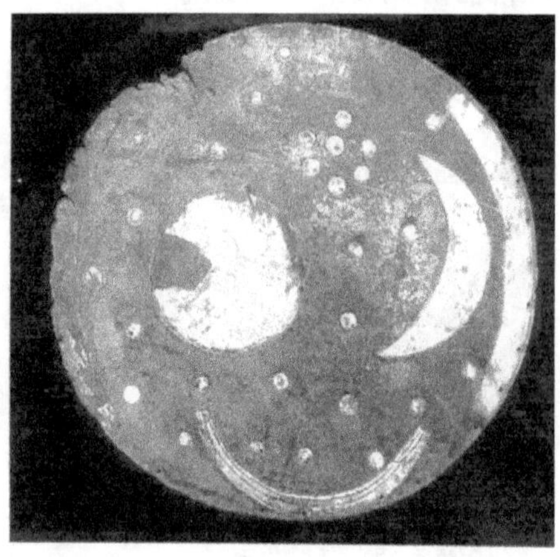

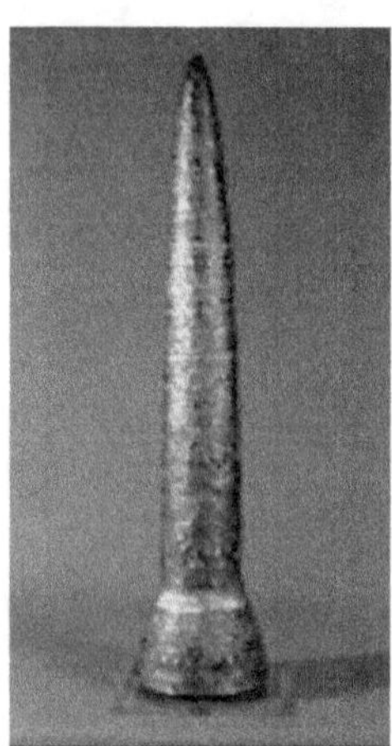

Mysterious ancient gold cone hats of Europe. They look like rockets and have flying saucers images as well as moons and suns. The priests wore these as hats.

This ancient Egyptian sculpture of Ahknenton has a religious ceremonial hat that resembles the gold cone and Easter Island.

Again, these disks, hats, gold, and obelisks all implicate and match flying saucer evidence and explain why they depict stars in space. It is already conquered by space faring beings that created our mysterious species to mine gold. Gold is crucial to explore space!

From 6000 B.C. A plate from Nepal, the decoration shows a saucer-like shape and a large-headed humanoid. These are craft seen by many thousands of people today all around the world.

UFO Coin, 1680. French Medal apparently commemorating a UFO sighting of a wheel-like object in Renaissance France.

The Yappese are the greatest of the Polynesian navigators. Our Hawaiian voyaging canoe "Hoku-lea" has a Yappese navigator. Since Yap is geologically unique in Micronesia, sedimentary in origin, all the rock is shale. Palau, about 700 miles southwest of Yap is predominately volcanically uplifted limestone created from ancient coral reefs. It is uniquely crystalline in nature. Voyaging to Palau by canoe, Yappese quarried this stone, risking their lives to get home with the largest coin. Many voyages were fraught with danger and adventure. The tougher the voyage, the more the money was worth! See hole in the center, like other ancient saucer/disk statues.

In Jabbaren, in the Tassali mountains, Algeria, south of the Hoggar. A 6 meter-high character with a large round decorated head. The massive body, the strange dressing, the folds around the neck and on the chest suggest some ancient time astronaut. A similar character is painted at Star in the Tassali, in the Cabro caves in France and in several other places. Some of them are much smaller and raise their hands towards a giant being, of non human appearance, sometimes these "round heads" beings seem to hover in the air. On right, an ancient painting ca. 1700 A.D. See how all the other ancient saucer art and photographs have a hole in the center. The biblical description of these fiery chariots, a circle within a circle!

Ufologist Bob Dean noticed a similarity between this UFO photographed by police officer Mark Coltrane in Colfax, Wisconsin on the 19th of April 1978 and the object in the ancient De Gelder painting.

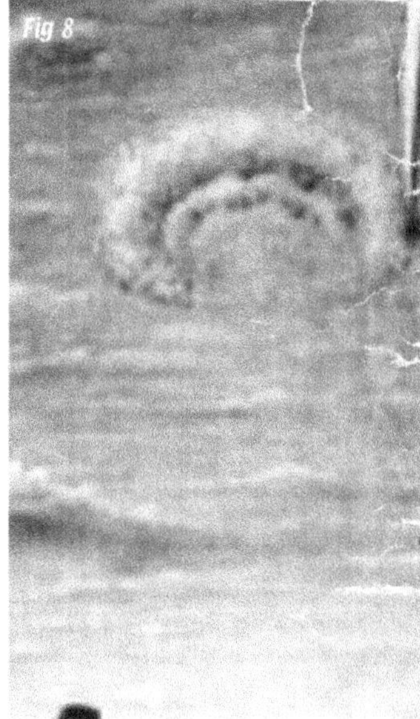

See similarity of photograph by Ed Walters on left to ancient painting of UFO on right.

Religious ancient disk and obelisk on left from China. See three dots at top of obelisk. Does this represent atomic propulsion of today's rockets? Ancient clay disk on right from Turkey.

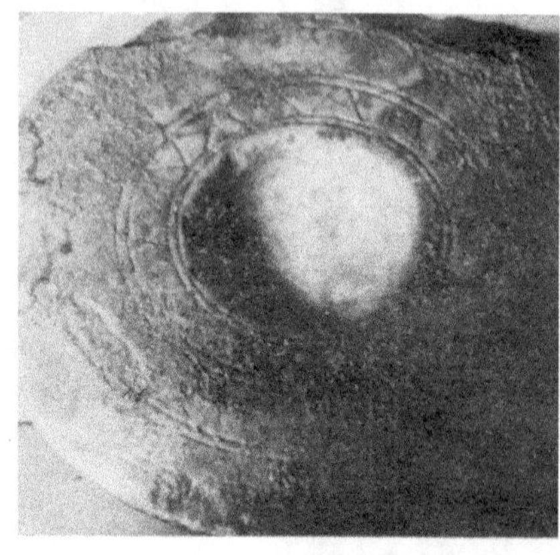

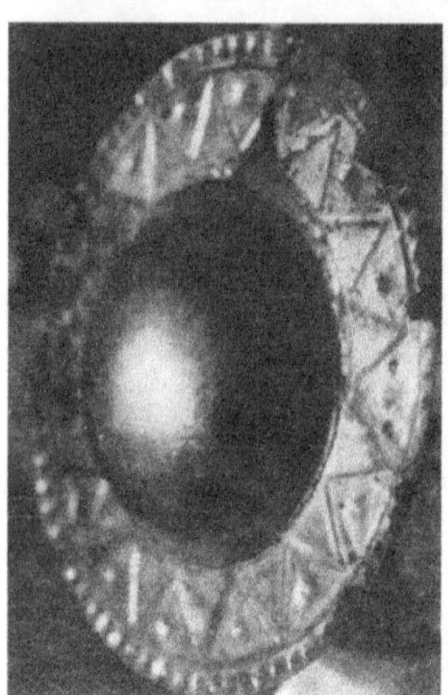

Ancient gold disk from Bogota, Columbia, matches clay mold from Turkey and flying saucers' shape.

See notches on outside perimeter! Important because it matches many others from other countries. All ancient.

Gold disk from Peru gold mine. See sperm and alien head and face. The center is full of atoms . . . again possibly evidence of atomic propulsion. There are faces in sun and stars. We are stardust/atoms/adams. Notice diamond infinity symbol.

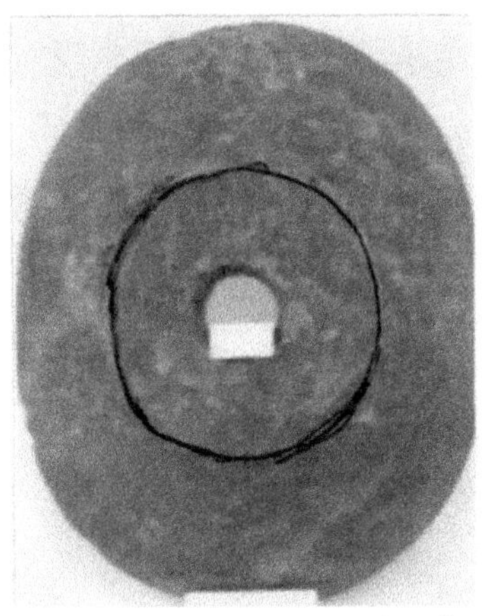

Ancient Yap stones "money stones" from the South Pacific. These are still used for money today, although it is rare. They look like the NASA tether saucer and all other ancient disks.

Ancient Chinese gold disk with rubies. It says "anywhere the sun shines, life will exist." This looks like a computer chip. The disk fits disk on Genesis probe.

Ancient cave art from Ubekestan. See notches like in Ohio and spirals like dropa stones. Besides, he looks like an astronaut. See atom symbol on jaw line.

This ancient disk was found in Ohio, my home state. It is a beautiful piece of evidence to support my theory. It has an eye in the middle of the "right" hand which is center of disk. This clearly represents the gods being in control, knowing all (omniscience) and controlling all (omnipotent). The rattlesnakes represent our deadly creation. The disks give them omnipresence.

Looks just like other UFOs of NASA!

These are dropa stones from Tibet and are circa 10000 years old. They were found deep in a cave with the remains of about 400 skeletons of little people with big heads. The island of Yap values an identical stone as money. They are called money stones. The largest ones measure up to 10 feet, and are made of polished white lime-stone. The whiter they are the more valuable. Now we see where the white thing comes from in religion. If these gods stay in spaceships they would be really white looking. The universal alien is the Roswell gray! If you don't buy this then buy an alien doll. It will be him!

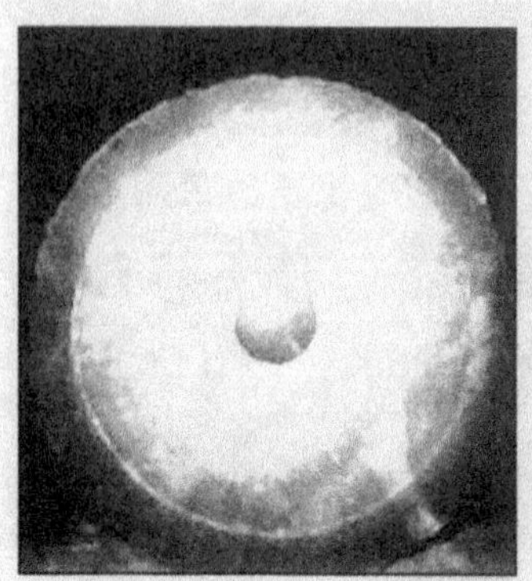

Dropa stone: Artifacts called Dropa stones, which bear an uncanny resemblance to the UFOs involved in the tether incident.

Last but not least, the Legend tells how they were attacked and eventually killed off by neighboring tribes because they were so "UGLY." Here again is evidence why they can't cohabit with us and how language comes full circle to support the evidence and answer the big question, "Where did they come from; What do they look like and why do they stay away?" They "dropped" out of sky according to legend and this is why the tribes they spawned are called Dropas. They still exist today and have physical attributes that resemble the alien. The Owl Man is your next answer and Cernes Giant the last of the three WWWs. Where, what, why!

Ancient stone carvings from Peru, "Ica stones."

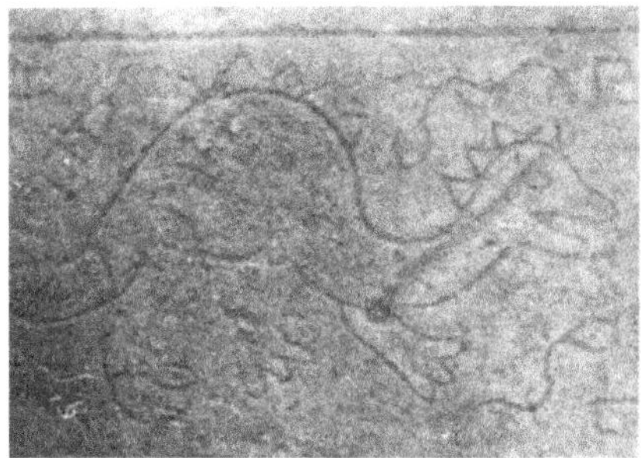

Notice sperm-like objects with DINOSAUR! Also amulet on right clearly shows big headed alien god above earth and not on it. The earth is gridded like we do today with latitude and longitude lines. How is any of this possible without space already being conquered by scientific beings?

Giant stones of Costa Rica. Again why? Does this prove knowledge of planets and atoms that would be important to space-traveling gods?

MONUMENT 4,
LA VENTA
2.26 m (7.41 ft) tall.
La Venta Park-Museum,
Villahermosa.

HEAD 10,
SAN LORENZO
1.8 m (5.9 ft) tall
Tenochtitlán Community
Museum, Veracruz.

These are six-foot giant heads of the Olmecs. Giant Heads! Notice DNA symbol and cross symbol of tenth planet on jaguar head at left. This mirrors sphinx. The right head has "six" claws on forehead and symbol of atom, cell or fertilized egg and flying saucers!

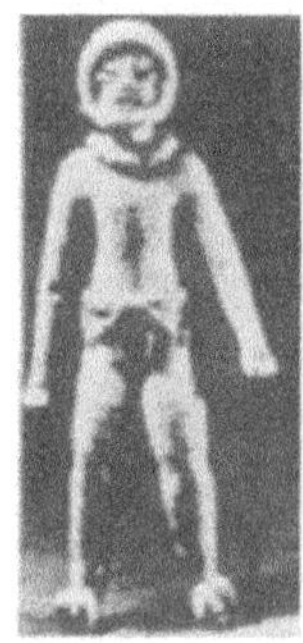

Maya god has gold halo above his obvious spacesuit. This makes it clear, gold is used to protect us in space! This evidence speaks for itself. These are ancient astronaut statues compared to a real one. The bottom one is identical. It was found in Peru and is 6,000 years old.

Also, these are airplane statues made of solid gold. This supports space travel's need for gold and proves gods are flesh and blood beings who have already conquered space!

THESE SPEAK FOR THEMSELVES AS WELL. They are all made of gold. From Egypt to Peru!

India

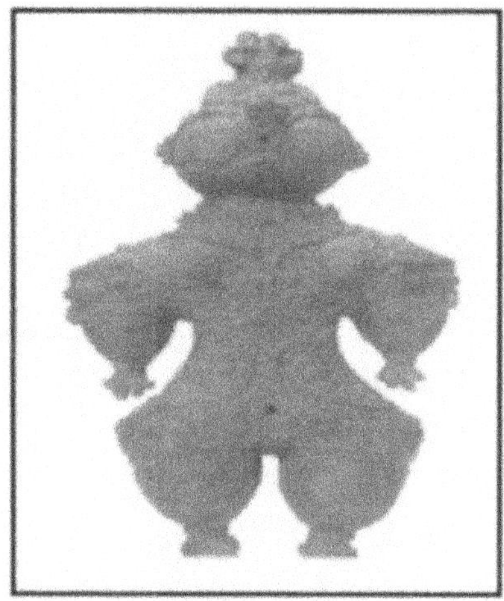

Look at alien eyes!

Turkey

Look at matching thrusters on obvious rocket. The head is missing on pilot.

More ancient statues

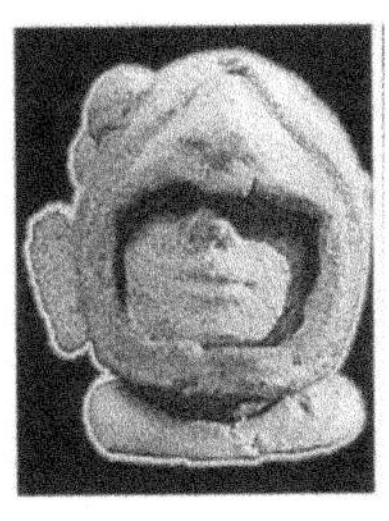

Ancient European astronauts!

Mexico Gold Star God
Alien head on DNA from sun bottom left hand.

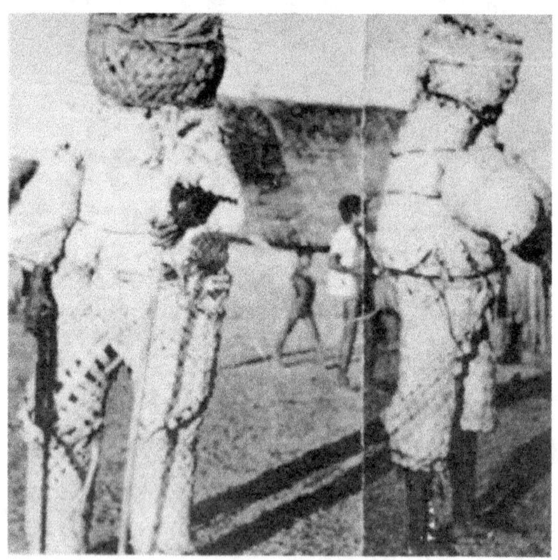

Brazil
Kayapo tribe still celebrates the legend of "Teacher from Heaven" Bep Kororot; this is his suit; stick, his "fire" stick. He made the villagers' weapons turn to dust when they tried to "attack" him. He helped them and then went to mountain top and disappeared in a cloud of thunder. They await his "Return!"

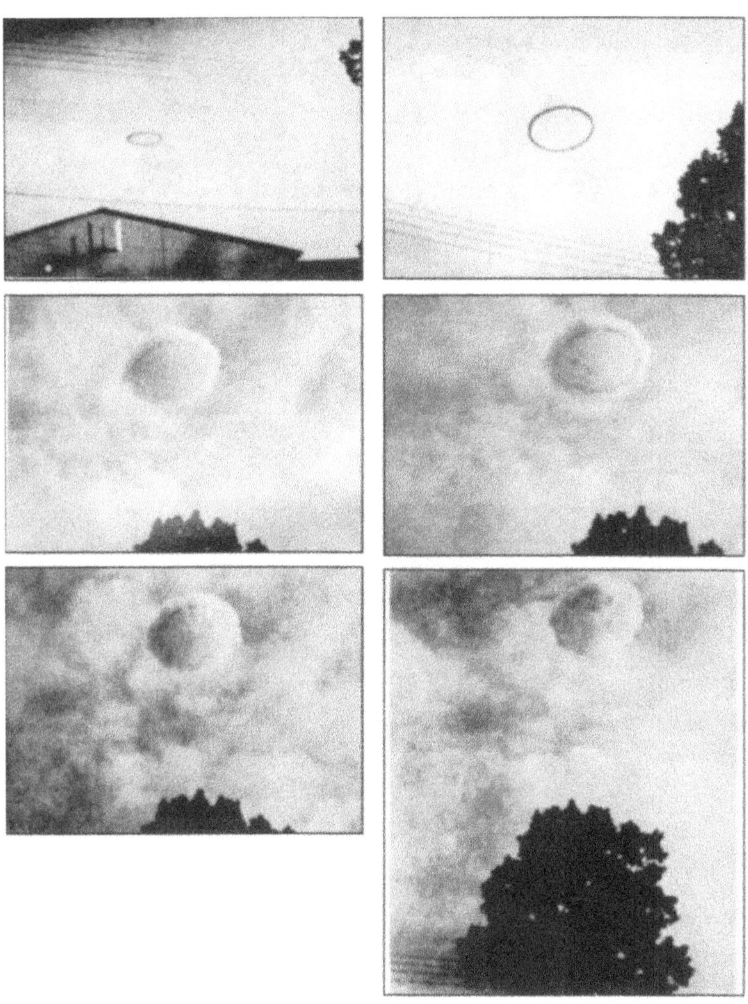

There are many legends of gods from the sky, in clouds that make thunder. The Kayopo story on the previous page mirrors that of Moses and his "ten commandments." They were also to teach us. Could this be the cloud of thunder? Actual photo taken by Army private in 1965. Eye witnessed by others and never explained!

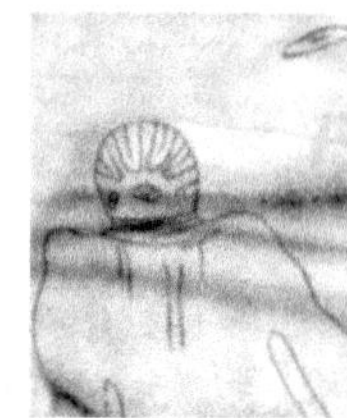

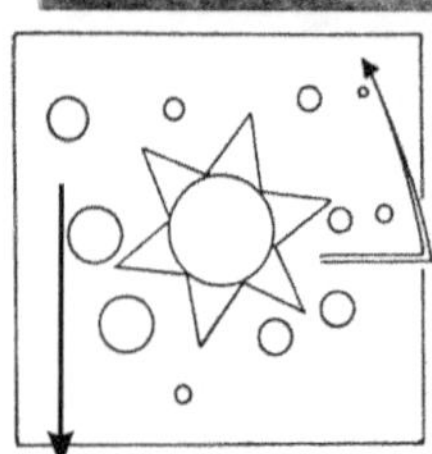

10th Planet

1. Notice cave grid looks like computer grid of space, and is flat like floating membrane. The membrane theory says space is infinite. It is a cyclical dance of creation and destruction. Also star of cave sculpture just like the Sumerian clay tablet below, and atom symbol. The clay tablet is dated circa 13000 years. The cave drawing is much older. They both show a 10th planet in our solar system. HOW?

2. The cave astronaut and gemini-looking capsule are also ancient. This is proof they existed before and supports my conclusion. Read on!

3. This is "Matching" irrefutable evidence that the ancients were communicating with space-faring people! Their absence makes it clear. Our mystery is what they look like!

4. See flying saucer in sky above astronaut! Again, a hole in the center!

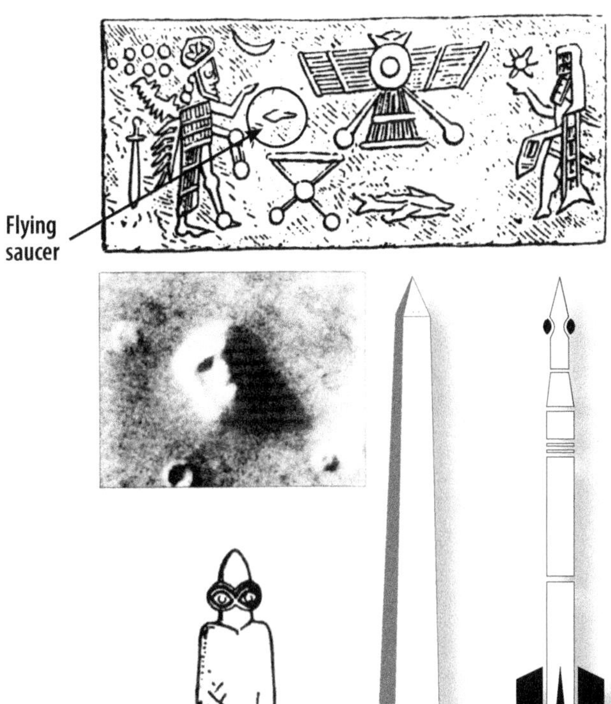

1. Notice the satellite on the clay tablet going from Earth (7th planet) to Mars (6th planet). It looks just like ones today. This tablet is also circa 13000 years. Also notice symbol for Mars matches atom and Jewish star. Is this proof that Mars could have had Man there first and we destroyed it with nuclear weapons? The "man" on mars is in a suit. Is it reason for contact?

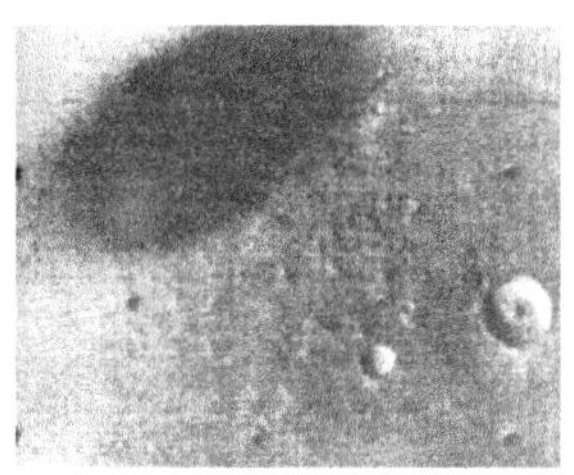

2. See how the helmet of Mars "man" on tablet matches our pictures of face on Mars.

3. Notice ancient satellite looks like alien head and eyes of nuclear missile. Egyptian obelisk matches nuclear missile. Egyptians called obelisks "rocketship".

4. See flying saucer monitoring earth on mars clay tablet.

5. This is a photo from phobos satellite sent to view mars moon phobos. It is irregular shaped and appears to be hollow. Could it be used as a space base on the inside? We think asteroids could be used this way as natural spaceships. This is the last picture it took before it was deemed "destroyed" by space debris. Looks like a flying saucer to me.

Three famous UFO incidents in the U.S. reported on the front page of each respective city's newspaper. The dates and places are on the last two. The first is Los Angeles and shows us shooting at it. It happened in Feb. 25, 1942. No wonder they don't cohabit with us. We never recovered it. Ten innocent civilians died from the shrapnel fallout!

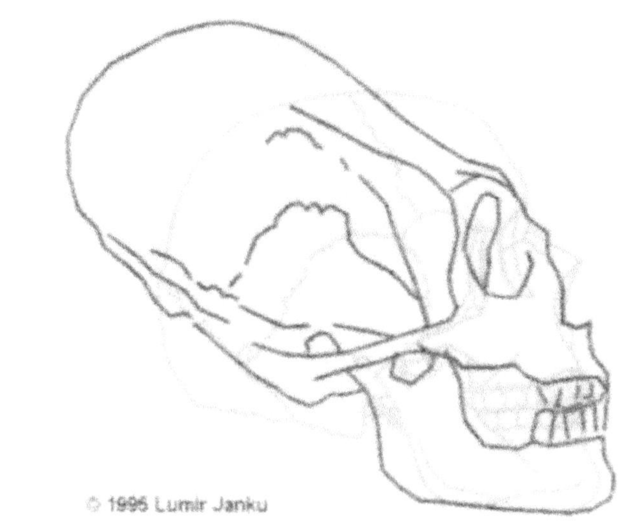

© 1996 Lumir Janku

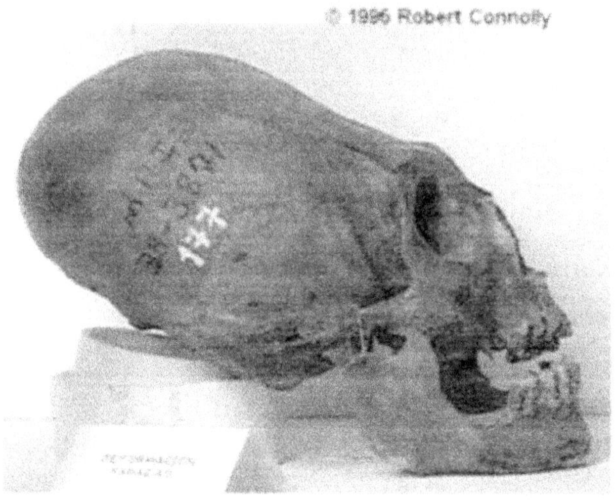

© 1996 Robert Connolly

Head molding was an ancient universal religious practice! Obviously, they were trying to imitate their gods' appearance.

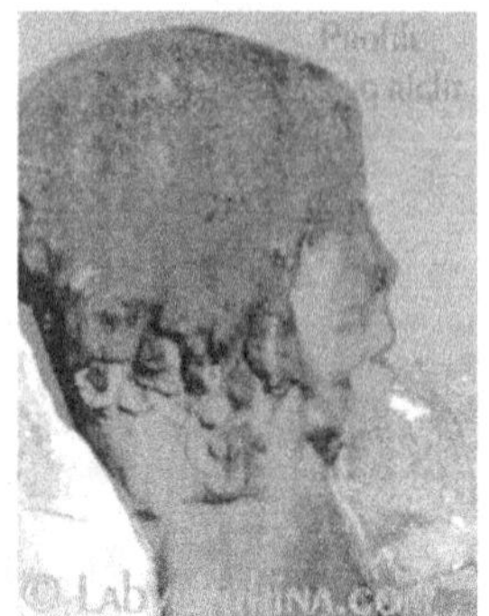

Ancient sculpture shows alien head and man's head together!

Ancient religious sculptures that match from three different continents!

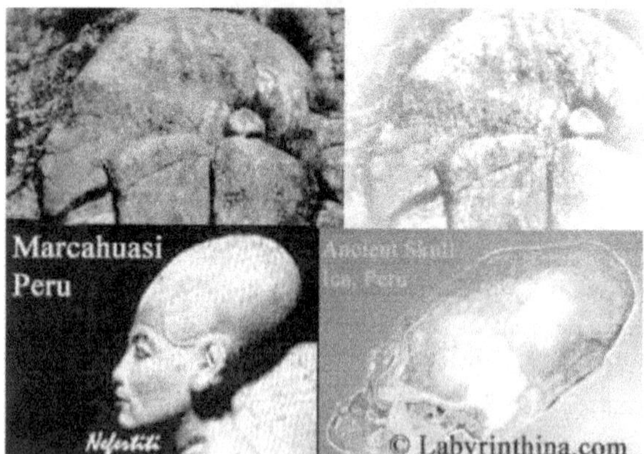

More matches! Ica, Peru has Ica stones that tell and show my theory. Alien-looking gods here with primitive man and dinosaurs creating our species, the mystery/modern man.

Ancient Egyptian relief "Stellae" of Ahknenton, Nefertiti, and children. Notice bald elongated heads and big alien eyes!

Egyptian papyrus clearly show Ahknenton's head without hat. It is alien looking like long limbs and fingers. The bald head is universal religious practice like ancient head molding!

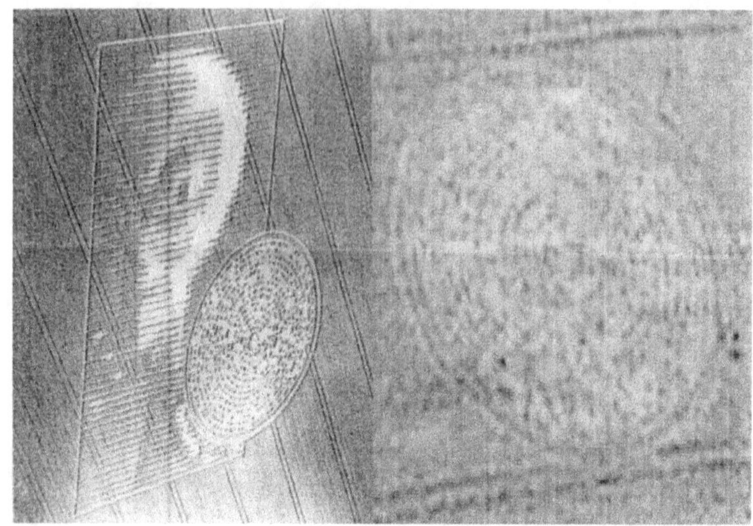

This crop circle has a coded message: "We are the good guys, not mankind!" This matches the quote by Yeshua when they called him good. "Only the Father in heaven is good," Luke 6:4. Is this proof that the aliens are the "father" and it is a plural term also. Yeshua said, "The Father and I are one." He also said we could be too! The evidence of an alien with a penis from Erich Von Daniken and the head of the mother goddess statue proves this universal story's facts.

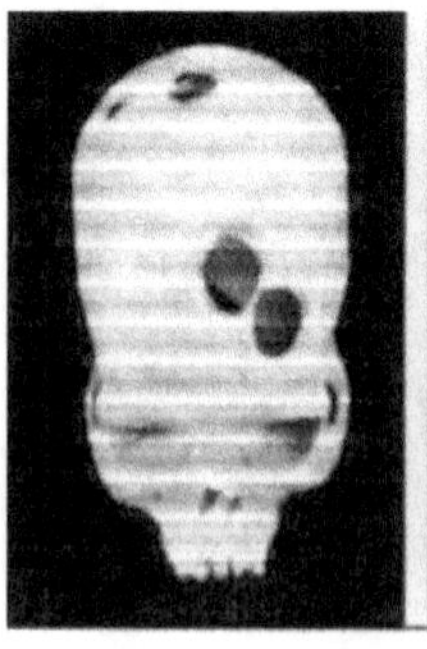
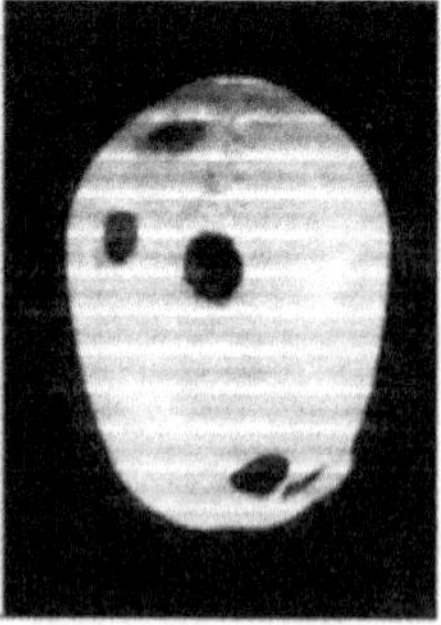

Ancient intrepanation skull! This was also universal religious practice. This could be how mental telepathy works. We are doing this today with cybernetics. Surgical tools found with skulls were made of gold!

Gold is the most ancient metal known to man and sacred to religion, everywhere. This information is provided by World's Leading Gold Mining Co.

History of Gold - Timeline

4000 BC	Gold is first known to be used in parts of Central and Eastern Europe.
3000 BC	The Egyptians master the arts of beating gold into leaf and alloying gold with other metals to variations in hardness and color. They also develop the ability to cast gold, using the lost-wa still used in today's jewelry industry. The Sumer civilization of southern Iraq uses gold to create a wide range of jewelry, often us sophisticated and varied styles still worn today.
2500 BC	Gold jewelry is buried in the Tomb of Djer, the king of the first Egyptian dynasty, at Abydos.
1500 BC	The immense, gold-bearing regions of Nubia make Egypt a wealthy nation, as gold become recognized standard medium of exchange for international trade. The Shekel, a coin originally weighing 11.3 grams of gold, is used as a standard unit of mea throughout the Middle East. The coin contained a naturally occurring alloy called electrum, v approximately two-thirds gold and one-third silver.
1352 BC	The young Egyptian King Tutankhamen is interred in a pyramid tomb laden with gold, his re an extravagant gold anthropoid sarcophagus.
1350 BC	The Babylonians begin to use fire assay to test the purity of gold.
1091 BC	Squares of gold are legalized in China as a form of money.
560 BC	The first coins made purely from gold are minted in Lydia, a kingdom of Asia Minor.
58 BC	Julius Caesar seizes enough gold in Gaul (France) to repay Rome's debts.
50 BC	The Romans issue a gold coin called the Aureus.
600-699 AD	The Byzantine Empire resumes gold mining in central Europe and France, an area undevel fall of the Roman Empire. Artisans of the period produce intricate gold artifacts and icons.
1100	1100 Venice secures its position as the world's leading gold bullion market due to its locatio trade routes to the east.
1284	Venice introduces the gold Ducat, which soon becomes the most popular coin in the world, so for more than five centuries. Great Britain issues its first major gold coin, the Florin, which is followed by the Noble, the A Crown, and the Guinea.
1511	King Ferdinand of Spain sends explorers to the Western Hemisphere with the command to '
1717	Isaac Newton, Master of the London Mint, sets price of gold that lasts for 200 years.
1787	First US gold coin is struck by Ephraim Brasher, a goldsmith.
1792	The Coinage Act places the young United Sates on a bimetallic silver/gold standard, definin Dollar as equivalent to 24.75 grains of fine gold, and 371.25 grains of fine silver.
1803	North Carolina site of first US gold rush. The state supplies all the domestic gold coined for the US Mint in Philadelphia until 1828.
1848	The California gold rush begins when James Marshall finds specks of gold in the water at Jc sawmill near the junction of the American and Sacramento Rivers.
1850	Edward Hammond Hargraves, returning from California, predicts he will find gold in Australi week. He discovers gold in New South Wales within one week of landing.
1859	The Comstock Lode of gold and silver is discovered in Nevada. As a result, Nevada is made years later.

Oldest gold mines found in Africa civilization traced from NE Africa science traces our origin to hominid they named "Eve."

Capsule bearing solar secrets

By PAUL FOY
Associated Press

SALT LAKE CITY — In a harrowing feat high over the Utah desert Wednesday, two helicopter stunt pilots will try to snatch a floating space capsule that holds "a piece of the sun" and bring it safely down.

Their biggest fear: What if they flub it on live TV?

And that's entirely possible. The pilots rate it 8 or 9 on a difficulty scale of 10.

"It's like flying in formation with a giant floating jellyfish," says pilot Dan Rudert.

The stuntmen will be trying to hook the 400-pound Genesis capsule as it hurtles 400 feet a minute. Inside it are fragile solar wind particles — so small they're invisible — which scientists hope will reveal clues about the origin of our solar system.

The biggest challenge, pilots say, will be flying at 40 mph almost a mile above the desert without visual reference points to judge distance or speed as they close in with hook and cable.

The helicopter pilots will have five chances to snag the capsule in midair. Military pilots were unavailable for a mission that required them to commit to a task six years in the future. The civilian pilots have replicated the retrieval without fumbles in dozens of practice runs, but are terrified of failing as NASA television broadcasts a worldwide feed.

If they miss and the Genesis capsule hits the ground hard, scientists say they'd have to spend months sorting through broken jewelry-studded disks holding the tiny solar wind particles.

There are other opportunities for the $260 million mission to go awry, too. For NASA engineers a white-knuckle moment will be when the capsule must be steered through a "keyhole" high in the Earth's atmosphere. If the experts at California's Jet Propulsion Laboratory can't line up the precise entry and angle, Genesis will be waved off on an elliptical orbit of Earth, and another attempt would be made in six months.

The Genesis mission marks the first time NASA has collected and returned any objects from farther than the moon, said Roy Haggard, Genesis' flight operations chief and CEO of Vertigo Inc., which designed the capture system.

Together, the charged atoms captured on the capsule's disks of gold, sapphire, diamond and silicone are no bigger than a few grains of salt, but scientists say that's enough to reconstruct the chemical origin of the sun and its family of planets.

Scientists will keep busy for five years after Genesis completes its ride to Earth. It will take at least six

This clearly shows our need for gold in space as well as other "precious" metals and gems. This explains religion's description of the same in heaven/space. After all, religion is universally anti-wealth.

RELIGION IS HISTORY!!!
MISSING LINK PROOF!

The alien skull shows the obvious mix between primitive man and himself producing us. We are the mystery! Religion began approximately 200,000 years ago when our big headed species started burying the dead and making artwork! This coincides with my theory like many others (Erich von Daniken and Alan Alford) that theorize intelligent beings from the sky manipulated primitive man and created this missing link in skull growth. The evidence shows that these religious gods are bigger headed than us and look like the stereotypical Roswell gray alien! This mix of their large head and primitive man's smaller one caused ours to jump the normal growth of evolution. Primitive man remained so for many millions of years without any evolution in knowledge or much change in skull size. The only logical explanation for the missing link and inexplicable sudden attainment of knowledge is religion itself. Not slow evolution, but a sudden scientific creation. The fossil evidence supports this reality! Religion is from Heaven or the sky! It is universal in the creation stories; it is clear that we are created to worship them or work for them. It is universal. This work or "purpose" can be traced directly to our first order of business. It was and is gold. It is universal. Gold is important for space travel. We are creating robots to assist in our space travels, which is only made possible with gold! This is universal! Even the robot itself is mostly composed of gold. It is the most resistant protector to the extreme conditions of space. The gold halo is the universal god symbol which is above the head. All gods are depicted as being able to fly. I am presenting the following religious symbols and their matching scientific counterparts as evidence to prove the creation of man was and is a scientific one. I propose that our true purpose is religion's pre-destined will; their pre-determined plan for us. Our true purpose is why they stay away on purpose. Please enjoy the exciting conclusion to my story. See for yourself how science is revealing an unfolding pre-determined plan for mankind that mirrors religion itself. Science today matches religion replacing the spirit-magic god with the alien!

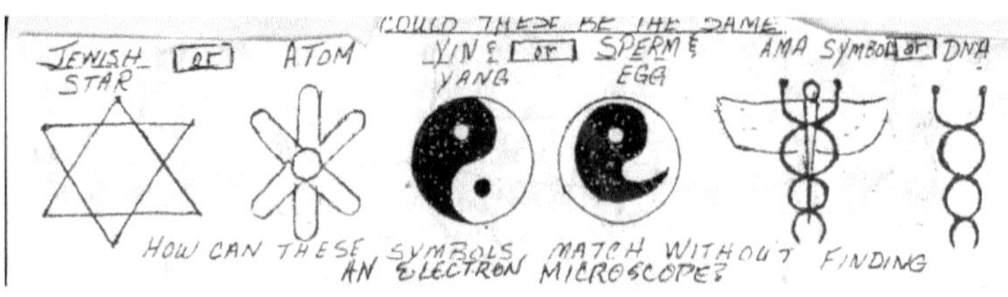

SYMBOLS:

Matching Themes:

Religion	**Science**
Omnipresence	Space Program
God is Infinite	Atom is Infinite
Creation/Man	Robots
Saving Life	Improve/Saving Man's Life
Multiply	Ensure Propagation of Species
Manipulating Age	Genetics for Manipulating Age
One Mind	Evidence Rules
Levitation	Anti-Gravity
Mummification	Cryogenics
Mental Telepathy	Cybernetics
Spirit	Holograms
Disappearing	Invisibility/Teleportation
Mystery™	Biorhythm Feedback

I'm sure there are many more. So please read on as I "have" to get to work! I'm sure you'll get the point. I propose that religion is not only the best evidence that space is already conquered, but tells us plainly the answer to Fermi's paradox: "Why don't they contact us?"! The world just hasn't come together to scientifically answer it. But of course we all know the world is just now global and capable of destroying itself. These are the two pre-requisites for the end to be ushered in. Coincidence? Our true purpose explains their silence and the reason they stay away on purpose. It is for the good of science. However, this is the end of their tortuous silence. It is the only way to save our planet. It is the next step in their plan. The two witnesses torture the world with their prophecy! Our species is the most unnatural self-destructive species in the universe. Get ready for contact. The "Regeneration of Man", Second Coming, Mayan Golden Age.

DNA similarities make world seem smaller

Survey says any two people 99.9 percent identical

By LEE BOWMAN
Scripps Howard News Service

Although everyone's genetic makeup is unique, scientists have found that populations from different parts of the world still share more genetic similarities than had been thought.

The results of a computer analysis of DNA from individuals representing 52 populations around the globe, published today in the journal *Science*, make up the largest such global survey of genetic diversity, and should help studies of ancient human migrations.

Those surveyed were broken into <u>five</u> regions: Africa, Eurasia, East Asia, Oceania and the Americas. Differences among individuals within those groups accounted for 93%-95% of genetic variety, according to the international team led by Marcus Feldman, a professor of humanities and sciences at Stanford University.

Compare the genetics of any two people, and the matchup will be about 99.9% identical. The research team accurately pinpointed the ancestral content of virtually every individual from Africa, East Asia, Oceania and the Americas. ■

1. How could Hopi medicine man know of five races, let alone the alien god?
See illustration on the next page.

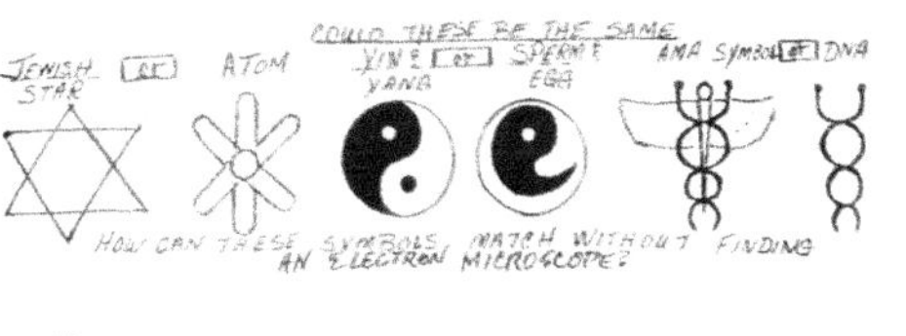

Alien statues found along banks of Jordan River 10,000 years old

2. Notice alien head on mother goddess statue. This supports what gods look like in Genesis 6:4. Statue dated circa 5000 years old found in Jerusalem, Israel.

3. Notice asexual organs on alien statue. This confirms Yeshua's description of angels and explains why they don't give their hand in marriage. They must be androgynous.

Mother goddess statues represent the inevitable separation that was to occur. According to religion mankind is predestined. It happened because the "sons of gods" thought the daughters of men were pretty. Their "giant" offspring became men of great renown and all wickedness spread all over the earth. This exemplifies their lust for power due to their obvious oneness in looks and small size. And they must have considered themselves ugly. It took place during the mysterious time frame, of the last ice age approximately 13,000 years ago up to the beginning of the Jewish calendar, 4000 BC (6,000 years ago). These are found all over the earth. The alien headed one is from Israel circa 8000 years old. The round headed one is 30,000 years. It is called the Venus of Willendorf. The asexual alien statue was found along the banks of the Jordan River. Notice the circles as if they knew about chromosomes and DNA. These as all scientists agree were religiously important and found in every household. I theorize that like the pyramids and Easter Island giants they were left to stand the test of time to tell us what their gods look like and where they are, Aliens and space.

The Cerne's Giant tells us why they couldn't cohabit with their creation of modern man (we kill for sex) and when they will return. (Three humps on club indicate an impending nuclear disaster. Atom has three parts.) The Owl Man tells us where their gods live and what they look like, space and aliens. It has a hummingbird which represents fertility pointing at it. Count the appendages and see connection to biblical number of man 666 and five races. The Hopi prophecy again shows us an alien god (big headed guy) saving the earth from destruction and recycling the majority of man up, obviously to another planet. Again how did the shaman know of the five races of man let alone an alien God? Notice similarity of box carrier to today's truck trailer. Feather on head indicates gods' ability to fly. See saucer attached to his arm.

The Five Faces of Man

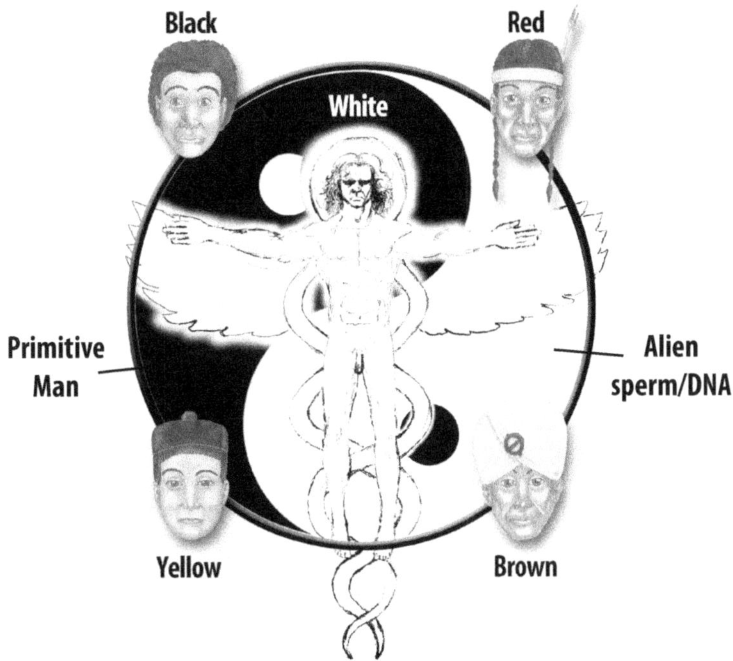

The different colors and facial structures indicate the competition to make the "prettiest" human. This "prettiest" factor is evident in Genesis 6:4 and the fall of the angel story!

Looks give us power over one another. All religions have a fall from heaven and earth being one, void and without form, to being separated. The gods/angels live in space—Earth becomes prison. This resulted from a power struggle. The biblical account gives us two creations. Nature created primitive man and then the gods/angels/aliens scientifically created modern man as a worker. Modern man is the mystery. The evidence universally points to mining gold. This started 100,000 years ago and continues to this day! The matching yin and yang and AMA symbol to the science symbols of the sperm/egg and DNA reflects our scientific creation. Even the biblical account describes a scientific process both for the man and the woman. The woman's creation is from man and he is anesthetized. Ultimately, I theorize two ongoing infinite creations: Nature's gods/angels/ white sperm/DNA and us from primitive man/black sperm/DNA. We are the mystery!

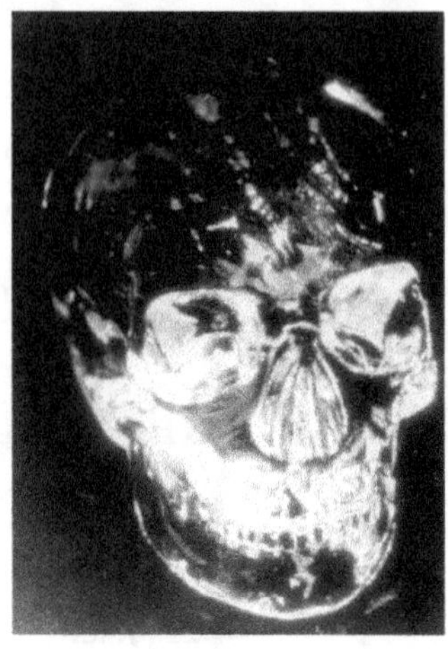

One of thirteen Mayan quartz crystal skulls. They are anatomically perfect, ancient and show no tool marks. Legend has it that they hold information that will solve our mystery which is where are the people/gods who made us and them? This crystal today is used for its electrical conduciveness "piezo electricity" and storage of information on computer chips.

This is where I propose they are. This is a statue from Easter Island that is looking up and appears to have a flying saucer on top of his head. They are in these religious fiery chariots of the sky.

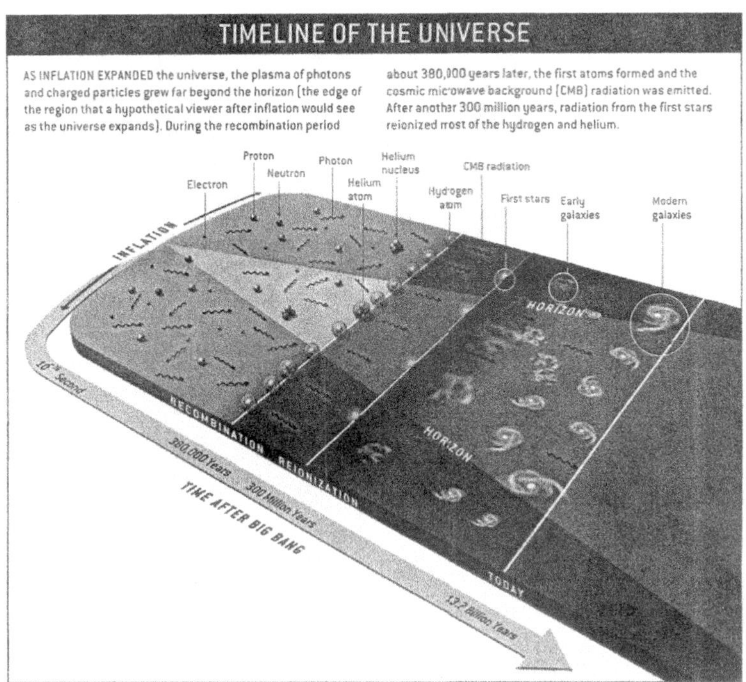

This is a perfect example of macrocosm science. The smallest parts mirror the whole. Atoms, photons, solar systems galaxies all resemble the universe itself. It is mostly space. The ancient geometry supports this theory/reality. I was amazed at how much a woman's egg looks like the sun (magnified) and when the sperm penetrates it the outer shell grows a green growth that becomes the placenta. The earth would only grow green vegetation from photon penetration. Photons look like sperm. Atoms look like suns, these look like eggs! Anyway, The problem with a beginning to our universe is that it is infinite. Only matter has a "beginning and ending". But this is an oxy-moron because atoms make matter and though one form ends it doesn't stop existing, another one just begins. This is all about image! Mind over matter and to be free of matter constraints, we must free ourselves from the matter. For space travel/freedom it is literally what we have to do. Free ourselves from the inevitable invisible eater of matter. GRAVITY! Matter itself. Does all this really matter? To be free it does. Flying is the ultimate freedom!

Exhibit 9

HERE is the proof of fraud. The Jehovah Witness acknowledge Yahweh & Jehovah as the same but don't call themselves Yahweh witnesses. Most importantly they don't recognize that Jeshua is the correct Translation from Yeshua. It is in the book of EZRA 3rd chapter (verse 2). It is from Yeshua. Why isn't it the same in the N.T.. It is easy to prove that Jesus, Jehovah, James, and Christ are all fraudulent, added words. (Why don't all Hebrew words have truly english equivalents?) We even have the correct names in the bible, that is if you accept the changing of Y's to J's. In this case with the Jehovah's witnesses, they actually choose Jehovah over Yahweh! The Four correct translations that are in the bible are Joshua, Yahweh, Jacob, & Messiah. Please hold them accountable for accuracy. This is not interpretation.
Sincerely,
Mike Brumfield

PROOF !!!

WHOA!

Chapter 24

Chapter 2[5]

The following is a clipping from the publication *You Can Live Forever in Paradise on Earth* (page 44):

44   YOU CAN LIVE FOREVER IN PARADISE ON EARTH

Yet, should we use God's name, even though we may not be saying it exactly the way it was originally pronounced? Well, we use the names of other persons in the Bible, even though we do not say them in the way the names were pronounced in the original Hebrew. For example, Jesus' name is pronounced "Yeh'su" in Hebrew. Likewise, it is proper to use God's name, which is revealed in the Bible, whether we pronounce it "Yahweh," "Jehovah," or in some other way common in our language. What is wrong is to *fail* to use that name. Why? Because those who do not use it could not be identified with the ones whom God takes out to be "a people for his name." (Acts 15:14) We should not only know God's name but praise it before others, as Jesus did when on earth.—Matthew 6:9; John 17:6, 26.

A GOD OF PURPOSE

Although it may be hard for our minds to understand, Jehovah never had a beginning and will never have an end. He is the "King of eternity." (Psalm 90:2; 1 Timothy 1:17) Before he began to create, Jehovah was all alone in universal space. Yet he could not have been lonesome, for he is complete in himself and lacks nothing. It was love that moved him to begin to create, to give life to others to enjoy. God's first creations were spirit persons like himself. He had a great organization of heavenly sons even before the earth was prepared for humans. Jehovah purposed for them to find great delight in life and in the service he gave them to do.—Job 38:4, 7.

When the earth was prepared, Jehovah placed a couple, Adam and Eve, in a part of the earth already made into a paradise. It was his purpose that they have children who would obey and worship him, and who would extend that paradise all over the earth. (Genesis 1:27, 28) As we have learned, however, that grand purpose was interfered with. Adam and Eve chose to disobey God, and his purpose has not been fulfilled. But

24. (a) To be consistent, why is it proper that we use God's name? (b) In view of Acts 15:14, why is it important to use God's name?
25. (a) What things about God may it be hard for us to understand? (b) What moved Jehovah to begin creating?
26. Why can we be certain that God's purpose for the earth will be fulfilled?

---

1. "Where is God?" is the $64,000 question. I thought God is omni-present! That means everywhere like the atom! They say he's all alone in space!

2. They say he's not lonesome but he's all alone. Then they say he creates for others. That's loneliness.

3. Finally they say he creates a heavenly organization of "spirit" sons like "himself". Why not daughters? And now they skip the fall of the angels story.

The following is a clipping from *Awake!* February 8, 2004 (page 19):

ble admonishes: "If you continue showing favoritism, you are working a sin."—James 2:9.

As science and technology advance, there are many new findings and theories about the human body. It is natural to be fascinated by these concepts. Still, Christians do well to let the Bible—not human theories—guide their thinking. In all walks of life, Christians need to "make sure of all things" and "hold fast to what is fine."—1 Thessalonians 5:21.

Awake! February 8, 2004   19

4. Last but not least. This is the proof that "religion", at least the Jews, make these angels and god "spirit" not flesh and blood. This is the ultimate cover-up. What if they come back and are the aliens? WWYD?

5. Proof that the J.W.'s discredit science! And ironically the scripture above James 2:9 makes their god a hypocrite. He has a favorite, yet forbids it. The chosen race of the Jews. No wonder people revere the Jews!

6. Finally they say the "Devil" is working through the U.N.! Don't they want a United Earth?

Modern-Day "Encounters"
With Angels and Aliens

Many people today claim that they have seen angels and spoken with them. Others say that they have had contact with aliens from other worlds. The book *Angels—An Endangered Species* lists the similarities between these accounts, claiming that both may have a common explanation.* Following is a summary of some similarities listed in the book.

1. Both angels and aliens come from other worlds.

2. Both are advanced life-forms, either spiritually or technologically.

> * The explanation common to both is that wicked spirits, or demons, are evidently behind many such "encounters." As the Bible says, "Satan himself keeps transforming himself into an angel of light." (2 Corinthians 11:14)—See *Awake!* July 8, 1996, page 26.

3. The friendly variety are youthful and beautiful in appearance, and they are kind and full of compassion.

4. Both have little trouble with language, speaking clearly in the language of the listener.

5. Both are masters of flight.

6. Appearances of both angels and aliens are accompanied by brilliant light.

7. Both appear fully dressed, commonly in either robes or close-fitting tunics. White or blue are favorite colors.

8. Both are usually the same height as humans.

9. Both express concern about the plight of humanity and the planet.

10. The evidence of both alien and angelic encounters is the testimony of the beholder.

★ ANSWER

Awake! November 22, 1999   5

Erich von Däniken

to count the pages of his metal library, but I accept his estimate that there might be two or three thousand.

The characters on the metal plaques are unknown, but if only the appropriate scholars were told of the existence of this unique find now I am sure that they could be deciphered comparatively quickly in view of the wealth of possibilities for comparison.

No matter who the creator of this library was, nor when he lived, this great unknown was not only master of a technique for the "mass-production" of metal folios in vast numbers—the proo[f] there—he also had written characters with wl[...] he wanted to convey important information beings in a distant future. This metal library w[as] created to outlast the ages, to remain legible f[or] eternity.

Time will show whether our own age is seriously interested in discovering such fantastic, awe-inspiring secrets.

Is it prepared to decipher an age-old work even if it means bringing to light truths that might turn our neat but dubious world picture completely upside down?

Do not the high priests of all religions ultimately abhor revelations about prehistory that might replace *belief* in the creation by *knowledge* of the Creation?

Is man really prepared to admit that the history of his origin was entirely different from the one which is instilled into him in the form of a pious fairy story?

(handwritten:) CALLED RELIGION'S SPIRIT WORLD!

10

This is why we must prove religion's origin. The Jehovah Witnesses are not helping to make peaceful contact! They don't even realize that their answer proves mankind is religion's devil and reincarnation! (Keeps transforming).

A ridiculous depiction of God by Jehovah's Witnesses. Sadly, this is universal. Religion is anti-wealth, making this even more insulting.

How to identify true religion

What good fruit should true religion produce?—Matthew 7:17.

Using science to prove God and make themselves look ridiculous with their quote, which disproves their God. (read about this in my story)

Could I be this Michael and the war about our evil species? Notice Tibetan religion's heavenly war also involves one third being rebellions! Their Sixth Stanza reads like modern science. The final admonition is to learn the "correct" age of the "small wheel." This is the atom and us. We are atoms/adams "appearing and reappearing continuously."

Atoms are infinite!

stars of God: I will sit also upon the mount of the congregation, in the sides of the north."

But we also find an unmistakable reference to strife in heaven in the New Testament. Revelation xii, 7–8, reads:

"And there was war in heaven: Michael and his angels fought against the dragon: and the dragon fought and his angels,

"And prevailed not; neither was their place found any more in heaven."

Many of the ancient documents of mankind mention wars and battles in heaven. The Book of Dzyan, a secret doctrine, was preserved for millennia in Tibetan crypts. The original text, of which nothing is known, not even whether it still exists, was copied from generation to generation and added to by initiates. Parts of the Book of Dzyan that have been preserved circulate around the world in thousands of Sanskrit translations, and experts claim that this book contains the evolution of mankind over millions of years. The Sixth Stanza of the Book of Dzyan runs as follows: *Like Sixth day creation in Bible*

"At the fourth (round), the sons are told to create their images, one third refuses. Two obey. The curse is pronounced . . . The older wheels rotated downward and upward. The mother's spawn filled the whole. *There were battles fought between the creators and the destroyers, and battles fought for space;* the seed appearing and reappearing continuously. Make thy calculations, o disciple, if thou wouldst learn the correct age of thy small wheel."

Satyr-comedy-Aristophanes: <u>Lysistrata</u>

Greek ~~Philosophy~~ "scientist"

Socrates: 469-399 BCE
    Socratic method/dialectic method
    "The unexamined life is not worth living."
Plato: 429-347 BCE, the Academy *(scientists)*
    "Until philosophers are kings or the kings and princes of the world
    have the spirit and power of philosophy...cities will never cease from
    ill, nor the human race."
Aristotle: 384-322 BCE, the Lyceum -peripatetic
    "Plato is dear, but truth is dearer."

Albert Einstein "I wonder if nature did not always play the same game"

Erich Von Daniken "I theorize that Alien intelligences must have been the same as homo sapians or very much like him!"

 Mike Brumfield: "I theorize the Roswell alien is the scientific creator of modern man/homo sapiens everywhere in the universe for the "soul" purpose of power and working for/worshipping him!

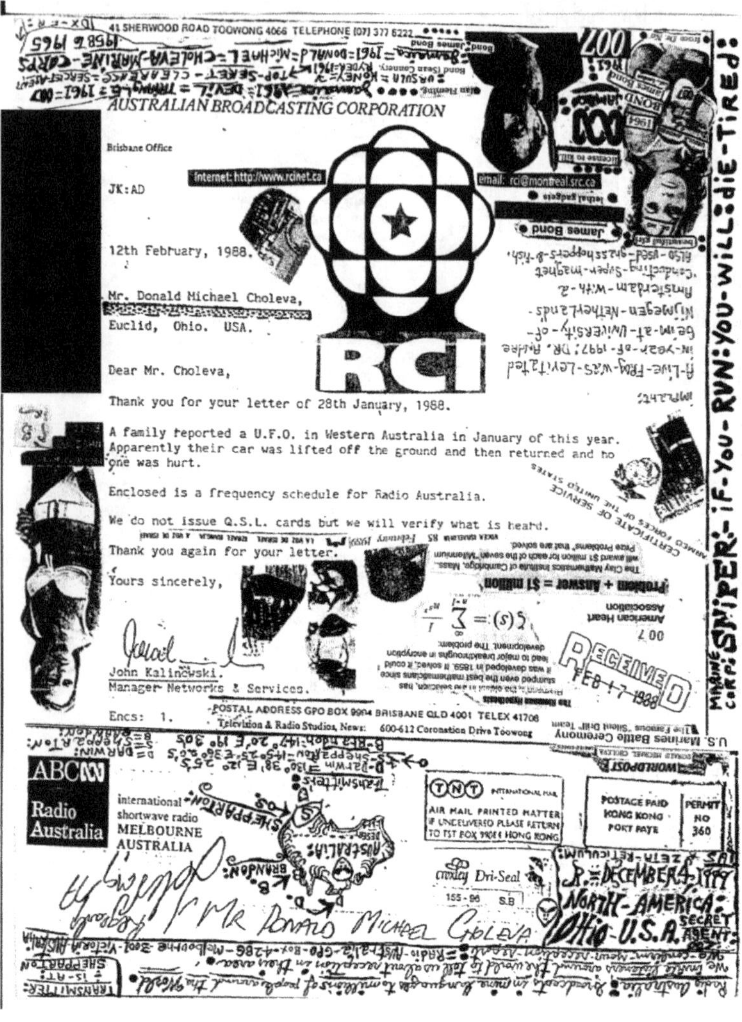

Blackened box in upper left corner had Marine Corps sniper stamp. This is a death threat of which I contacted the police. It came in the mail!

Clearly, scientists want cloak of invisibility

If they could only see a way to make it ...

By ANDREW BRIDGES
Associated Press

WASHINGTON — The key to creating a Harry Potter-like invisibility cloak lies in manmade materials unlike any in the Hogwarts School of Witchcraft and Wizardry, researchers say.

They're laying out a blueprint for turning science fiction into reality. And they say that, in theory, nothing's stopping them from making such a cloak.

Well, almost nothing. They still need to perfect the manufacture of those exotic materials with an ability to steer light and other forms of electromagnetic radiation around a cloaked object.

"Is it science fiction? Well, it's theory and that already is not science fiction. It's theoretically possible to do all these Harry Potter things, but what's standing in the way is our engineering capabilities," said John Pendry, a physicist at the Imperial College London. Details of a study that Pendry co-wrote are in Thursday's online edition of the journal Science.

"This is very interesting science and a very interesting idea, and it is supported on a great mathematical and physical basis," said Nader Engheta, a professor of electrical and systems engineering at the University of Pennsylvania who has done his own work on invisibility using novel materials called metamaterials.

Pendry and his co-authors also propose using metamaterials because they can be tuned to bend electromagnetic radiation — radio waves and visible light, for example — in any direction.

A cloak made of those materials would neither reflect light nor cast a shadow.

Instead, like a river streaming around a smooth boulder, light and all other forms of electromagnetic radiation would simply flow around it. An onlooker would appear to peer right through the cloak, with everything inside it concealed.

Early versions that could mask microwaves and other forms of electromagnetic radiation could be as close as 18 months away, Pendry said. He said the study was "an invitation to come and play with these new ideas."

"We will have a cloak after not too long," he said. ■

Invisibility is the Holy Grail of Science. Also, it is at the core of religion and the modern-day UFO phenomenon.

MODERN PHYSICS

THE BASIC ELEMENTS OF MATTER

What is **matter**?

Matter is anything that takes up space and has mass (or weight, which is the influence of gravity on mass). It is distinguished from energy, which causes objects to move or change, but which has no volume or mass of its own. Matter and energy interact, and under certain circumstances behave similarly, but for the most part remain separate phenomena. They are, however, inter-convertible according to Einstein's equation $E = mc^2$, where E is the amount of energy that is equivalent to an amount of mass m, and c is a constant, the speed of light in a vacuum.

In 1804, the English scientist John Dalton formulated the atomic theory, which set out some fundamental characteristics of matter, and which is still used today. According to this theory, matter is composed of extremely small particles called atoms, which can be neither created nor destroyed. Atoms can, however, attach themselves (bond) to each other in various arrangements to form molecules. A material composed entirely of atoms of one type is an element, and different elements are made of different atoms. A material composed entirely of molecules of one type is a compound, and different compounds are made of different molecules. Pure elements and pure compounds are often referred to collectively as pure substances, as opposed to a mixture in which atoms or molecules of more than one type are jumbled together in no particular arrangement. 341

People . . . please learn that matter is energy and infinite! This explains the $E = mc^2$ of energy. Atoms can be neither created nor destroyed!

and the second beast like a
and the third beast had a face
"If your days had not been shortened;
No flesh would be saved."
them six wings ab
they were full of eye
rest not day and night, say
Holy, holy, holy, Lord God
beasts, and in the midst of the elders, stood a Lamb as it had been
sat upon the throne.
The living creatures and elders
COULD THE JEWISH STAR BE . . .
THE ATOM!
WWYD
TIME HEALS ALL WOUNDS
12.20.01   12.20.01   12.20.01

Proof
Introducing Jeff and Mike they find it!!
Jeff gives you current flying saucer footage that
matches Johnny Cash sighting in 1980 & Easter Island (back cover)
Mike Brumfield REVEALS
Scientific Religous Evidence
"Why They Don't Show And When They Will"
More inside...
Jeff's
Johnny's
Matching Saucer's!
Real photo of
Johnny Cash in
1980
Solves Easter Island Mystery And More!
Famous Painting 1400 A.D.
of a Flying Saucer
Flying Saucer
Matches Also!
Man looking "UP"
at it
Close up View

HY THE BLANK DON'T THEY CARE?
VIDEO 2003
e were also shocked to look "UP" and see them!
d these ancient religious "chariots of fire"
eate religion's stories, "heavenly beings in the sky"
nd their universal halo symbol "UP"
ove their head? It is a saucer shape!
EADS OF EASTER ISLAND
LOOKING "UP"!
HIS EVIDENCE MATCHES
ncient Flying Saucer Statue

Letter to *UFO Magazine*, February 20, 2006, about Jeff's proposal to find flying saucers. They didn't bite, and we filmed them during trip. The still didn't bite even after contacting them with our footage to prove we found them!

Bill:
I have enclosed a video for you to review. I recently talked with you about the Johnny Cash photo and emphasized how this could garner serious attention for a huge breakthrough discovery. The flyer clearly shows a match between Jeff's flying saucer and the alleged hat of Easter Island. This also matches Johnny's saucer which is on the cover of the video. Please bear with the amateur quality of my video. My narration/explanation of why they don't show is one hour long. Then the 2003 video footage of Jeff's flying saucers begins. I also included the 1952 White House incident. This alone should demand attention. I will be coming to LA and approach the *Times* with my breakthrough discovery in man's quest for contact. The head of Easter Island is clearly looking up and has a flying saucer on top of its head. This answers the questions that Barbara Walter's just posed to all esteemed religious scholars of the Earth including the Dalai Lama, "Where is heaven?" My breakthrough religious scientific discovery of the world's largest ancient statue of a flying saucer confirms all ancient writings as well as today's space pursuit. Heaven is up, space is the final frontier. It is already conquered like religion confirms. The owl man of Peru shows us the same message. He is pointing up! The owlman and Easter Island statues are bald headed big-eyed statues like the Roswell alien. There are many depictions in ancient artworks of aliens and flying saucers that confirms this reality. I am sending also a cover of my latest book showing some of these that can't be refuted. I hope you will consider contacting me for an interview. We can't believe that nobody is taking this seriously. That is why we titled our next video "Why the Blank Don't They Care." I make it clear in the video why they don't show. The evidence speaks for itself. We are mining gold for them, since our beginning. Gold is important for space travel. Our creation is scientific and can't be stopped. There is no spirit magic and people get addicted to beauty of the flesh which gives us power over one another. The Easter Island statues all look the same. It would be great to have your magazine chronicle our journey on getting some attention for this discovery. We will prove that flying saucers are here now by videoing them together. This will happen after I leave LA on my return trip to Nashville. My partner Jeff lives in Phoenix and films them regularly. He promises me that we will see one. I believe him. Do you? Funny thing, that religion's universal contact story is about believing. We propose that this flying saucer evidence will answer that question. And yet, the story goes that most won't. We are entrenched in a spirit world belief system. Could religion be a direct result of primitive man's contact with flying saucers and aliens. They have both universal traditions, a gold halo symbol and bald heads.

Sincerely,
Mike

People, crimes and mysteries are solved today through the scientific method of matching evidence. The perpetrators of religion live in the sky. We are now videoing flying saucers everywhere and we now live in the sky! Could flying saucers and a real flesh and blood alien species have created religion as the matching evidence suggest? If you can open your mind to accepting evidence it is easy to "SEE" how advanced technologies would have created primitive man's spirit magic traditions. However, fortunately enough the foundation of his story though has never changed. These people live in the sky. The evidence does show "HEAVEN IS SPACE, UP!"

AND THIS IS THEIR SYMBOL . . . .

The gold halo above their head is their symbol! It looks like a flying saucer! What they look like is the ultimate evidence that will solve our mystery and Fermi's Paradox. The statues on the next page clearly answer the question of who and what primitive man's god looked like. Why they created our species is obvious. It also matches their story. They desired beauty of the flesh. This gives them "greatness" over one another. Coincidence? "Religion cover-up" is the title to my first book.

This is the "head/person" that should be under the gold halo. Funny how the book cover shows the shroud which looks like space beneath it. Because it exemplifies what the cover-up in religion is all about. What heaven's occupants look like? And where are they? The evidence says clearly that they are aliens UP IN SPACE! If you don't follow evidence or can't imagine a new discovery of an ancient relic that could solve our mystery, then please watch "The Planet of the Apes." The apes ignore scientific evidence over their religious stories of God creating them, just like my story today! Why the blank don't they care! Check out my video. Are we all addicted to outward beauty? Hell, yeah!!! Can't, couldn't do anything. I've always said instant creation/magic wasn't possible, but if it is, I guarantee it to be scientific. And then, it couldn't make this universe perfect. Babies are being raped. Finally, people . . . please answer for yourself why anybody would let this happen if they could stop it. I promise you, there's only one logical answer . . . they can't.

**Please ask yourself one question . . .
Do you like beauty of the flesh?**

**Oh, and by the way,
if you thought
What The Bleep Do We Know
was good, wait until
you see my next film . . .**

What the Blank Is Their Problem?

**This last picture will
"drive my point" . . .
home!**

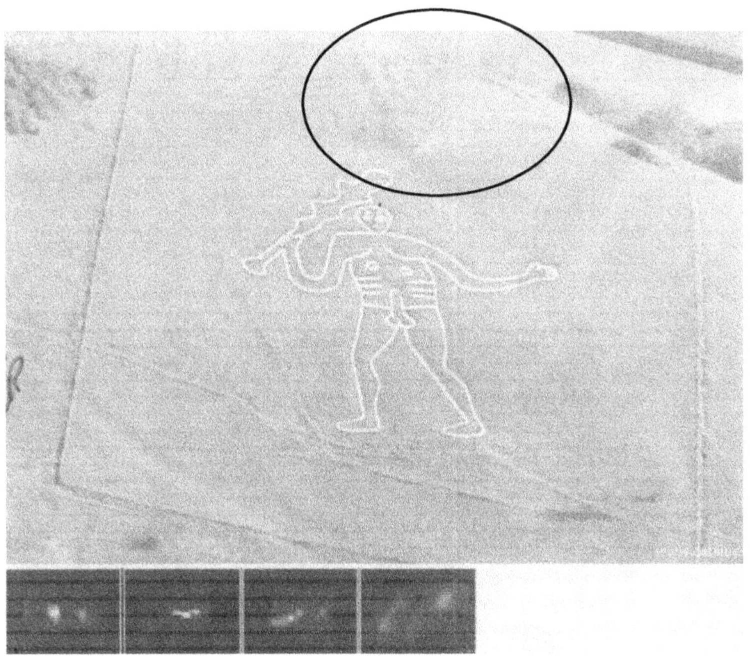

This is the Cernes Giant of Cerne, England. Legend has it that it is a Saxon god. My conclusion, based on the evidence I've presented, is that the god of primitive man is an alien and his fiery chariot is a flying saucer. The images below the giant are from video that I shot in Phoenix, Arizona, March 6, 2006. It is a flying saucer. It also matches the mound circled/squared above the head of this Cernes Giant/god. The most compelling matching evidence is the shape of the mound, a ring within a ring, and the bald head and big eyes of the giant. The craft matches my craft as can be seen at the following exhibit's website, and the head of this giant matches the aborigine alien-looking god, as well as all others. My last word on this evidence issue, to religious people and the rest of the world, is the bald-headed traditions of all religions and looking UP! This relief carving is another example of part alien/part man with a fiery chariot "UP" above his head!

Get the point!

UFO Performs Acrobatics Over Phoenix

3-15-6

3 witnesses observed the videotaping of a UFO performing aerial stunts so astonishing it made it on the Channel 3 News in Phoenix. Once again, Jeff Willes' constant skywatching pays off big time...

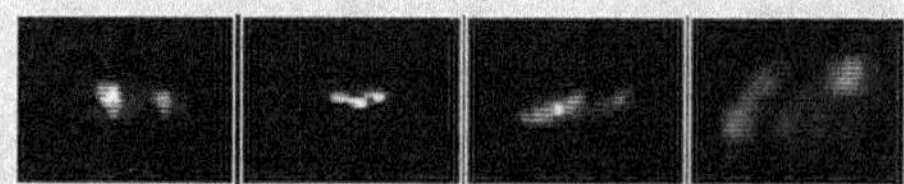

To view part of the video click here
(Windows Media Player file - wmv)

Report from Jeff Willes of NFO

"I was out in the back yard skywatching late on 3-6-06. At 12:00 am one of the others skywatching with me saw a UFO come up from the trees about a mile away and then go down again. We ran up to the top of the roof leaving our tripods on the ground, forgetting them in all the action. When we got on the roof we saw not one but two UFOs shooting way up in the sky and then coming back down behind the trees. The UFOs shot up and came back down 3 times. One of the craft would fly over upside down and then dive down. It did this 3 or 4 times. I took the tape to KYVK Channel 3TV here in Phoenix. They aired the footage on 3-10-06. They showed how the object flips over. I have been videotaping UFOs sense 1995 and have never seen anything like it."

Jeff Willes
www.ufosoverphoenix.com

I was the other witness along with Jeff and his wife. The daytime footage I shot is on the back cover of this book. I spent three days and videotaped well over ten flying saucers. Even the news reporter commented that the behavior of our saucer footage definitely proved it was not any kind of aircraft known to man. You can view the footage at **ufosoverphoenix.com**!